SEE YOU LATER MAYBE NEVER

PRAISE FOR SEE YOU LATER MAYBE NEVER

"This collection of linked stories is the welcome work of a mature writer. Dense with detail and nuance, the stories are fully-fleshed, satisfying, and time and time again will jolt the reader with recognition."

~ Sharon Butala, finalist for the Writers' Trust fiction prize for her collection *Season of Fury and Wonder*

"Follow the rich tapestry of memory on the footsteps of time. Lenore Rowntree's *See You Later Maybe Never* is entertaining and memorable, but first and foremost—a must read. An expedition for all."

~ Susan E. Lloy, author of *Vita*

SEE YOU LATER MAYBE NEVER

LENORE ROWNTREE

| N₁ | O₂ | N₁ |

CANADA

Library and Archives Canada Cataloguing in Publication

Title: See you later maybe never / Lenore Rowntree.

Names: Rowntree, Lenore Ruth, 1950- author.

Identifiers: Canadiana 20220265801 | ISBN 9781989689400 (softcover)

Subjects: LCGFT: Short stories.

Classification: LCC PS8635.O887 S44 2022 | DDC C813/.6—dc23

Printed and bound in Canada on 100% recycled paper.

Now Or Never Publishing
901, 163 Street
Surrey, British Columbia
Canada V4A 9T8

nonpublishing.com
Fighting Words.

We gratefully acknowledge the support of the Canada Council for the Arts
and the British Columbia Arts Council for our publishing program.

for
Merry Norah Ruth
and
Marion Silverthorn Bishop

— PART ONE —

THEN

— PART TWO —

BEFORE THEN

— PART THREE —

LATER

— Part One —

Then

LINE ON, LINE OFF

Vanessa eyes the knot at the end of the plank laid out on her workbench. She moves a hand plane along the grain, careful not to bruise the wood with her bracelet. A curl shaves back toward her face throwing up a pinch of scent. It makes her want to put her tongue on the streak of exposed pine, lodge a molecule of bitter pitch in the back of her throat.

The instructor at the front of the class makes the almost imperceptible dip of his head that signals he's about to talk. He's a compact man named Luke with hair the colour of the sawdust that comes up around the knot Vanessa is planing—brown with hints of gold. Her body straightens to listen as she watches a red glow emerge from the collar of his shirt, move up his throat, and into his cheeks.

"Everybody come and have a look at what Heather has done with her corners," he says.

Vanessa sets the plane down ready to move, but she waits. She doesn't want to be first up beside Luke, again. She wipes at the beard of shavings that hang from the front of her mohair sweater. A dumb choice for woodworking class, even if cerise does make her look younger. She knows from years in fashion this is the best colour for a cool-toned brunette like herself. She used to tell her salespeople, "Look at the pulse. If the veins are blue, the customer is cool."

When she starts to make her move, she gets hung up behind Ernesto working at the bench next to hers. His foot is up on his stool and his body turned into the aisle so there's no easy way around him. He's taken this moment to sip espresso from his thermos. He drinks slowly. By the time she's finally able to glide forward, she's so far back she can't see anything. She can only hear what Luke is saying.

"These brass guards Heather has put on her box are practical for a functional piece. She's done a fine job. Take a look and think about how you're going to finish your corners. Don't forget about the dovetail joint for those of you who can handle it."

Vanessa sees Luke hold something up in the air, but isn't sure what it is and doesn't dare venture forward to have a closer look. As she walks back to her station, she silently mocks the Heather-this-Heather-that of it all. It's only the second week and already she's sick of so much Heather. Why are the blondes always the centre of attention? Especially when Ernesto is clearly the most accomplished—though she can't blame Luke for not wanting to move in too close—wine and salami breath with overtones of coffee for sure. That much she can tell just by looking at his swarthy neck beard.

Vanessa's head is down close to the plank when she feels the heat of a body behind her. She thinks it might be Ernesto, so she doesn't look up and is startled to hear Luke's voice over her shoulder.

"Move the plane with more assurance."

Luke puts his hand on top of hers and together they glide along the plank in one smooth motion.

"That's better," he says.

He smells of pine. When she sneaks a sidelong glance she sees what she'd thought was a streak of grey in his hair is only specks of sawdust. His hand looks surprisingly boyish on top of hers, their fingers lightly interlaced, his tanned and hers almost translucent white. At the nearness of his youth, her hand makes an almost imperceptible movement of discontent. They both feel it.

"Easy," he says.

She smiles shyly and being unsure she can continue, takes her hand off the plane. When their eyes lock for a second, the strain is intense, as if the muscles behind her eyeballs might spasm. She looks down from his face and sees a faded insignia on his t-shirt: *Hart House, University of Toronto*. She keeps her eyes averted, gazes at his shoes while she digests this new information—he's educated. His eyes do look wise.

She convinces herself all over again that despite his youthful skin, he could be close to forty.

When Vanessa's husband Tom turned sixty-two, he'd taken the package the board offered for his twenty-five years in the trenches as a high school principal. A year later, Vanessa said she didn't want him to feel alone in this step, so she'd leave her work, too. But the truth is the colour and light in her job had dimmed the day she was told her *demographic* (read *age*) made her perfect for the newly created position of executive buyer. What this really meant is that she was no longer going to be the lead buyer for an exclusive retail chain, rather she was to take direction from a woman who was twenty years her junior and whose sensibility tended toward grunge with multiple piercings and tattoos.

Possibly, the decision to retire was made too hastily. Tom adjusted more easily than she did, though he spends a lot of his time walking Lucy, their adored King Charles spaniel. Vanessa at fifty-five had been too young, and she'd gone house-crazy in the year since. She misses traveling the world searching for fashions, haggling with exotic dealers and brokers, and she overfills her days with largely irrelevant community meetings and uninspiring courses.

For some reason, the description of the woodworking course had been different. It leapt from the calendar of options advertised in the newspaper—*build you own toolbox in just 8 weeks*. When she'd read the ad, she thought she could use the box to store the Japanese carving tools Tom had given her for her fifty-fifth birthday. The tools were something she'd said in passing she wanted, and he'd taken her seriously. At her birthday dinner, he'd said, "Nothing's too fine for you." What he hadn't said was that he'd been observing her unhappy spiral as she was being edged out of her job—something she hadn't acknowledged to herself at the time—and he'd grasped at the only thing that seemed to hold her amusement for more than a few seconds.

Most importantly, Vanessa knew she needed to build a box as proof she was actually doing something with her time. But she'd made a big mistake when she registered for the workshop. She'd taken the discount offered for early seniors. In joining that group, she'd made an honest effort to embrace the next stage, to stop shrinking back whenever Tom enveloped her in a bear hug of enthusiasm for their new life. Still, she felt dismayed when she arrived at the first class to see the giant red star beside her and Ernesto's names. Evidently, they were the only two who were over fifty-five. It's like the instructor had been warned: *watch out these two are dangerously old and should not be working with sharp objects*. The implication pissed her off.

After the first session, she was primed to drop out. It had taken two hours each way to do the bus-subway-bus shuffle from the house in Leaside to the workshop in Swansea. She'd come home at the end of it with a nose full of pine dust, an attitude as wet and tired as the mid-October day it was, and a hate-on for Toronto Transit. Then there'd been that difficult conversation with Tom.

"Why don't you find a closer workshop?" he asked.

"There isn't another one like it," she said.

"What's this class again?"

"It's not the class, it's the instructor."

"Well, what's so special about the instructor?"

When she signed up, she imagined someone more like Ernesto would be teaching. A stout, old-world man who'd spent too many years in the backyard tending grapes and staking tomato plants to have any sex appeal left. Instead it's the surprisingly arousing Luke, and she didn't know how to answer Tom. She was grateful when he left the question hanging to bend over and give Lucy an affectionate pat.

"Okay, Lucy and I will drive you next time. We'll walk High Park while we wait. Won't we old girl."

Lucy gave her head a shake and her collar rattled. She liked the attention.

Luke pauses at Vanessa's workbench. She stiffens. She hates that she can't feel relaxed around him.

"That's enough planing," he says. "Take a piece of medium sandpaper and see if you can straighten out that dimple. Look for the spirit in the wood."

"I'm trying," she mumbles.

It's week four already and she's barely ready to glue. Her hands still feel like two clubs when she works. The week before, Ernesto, already on to his second box, had stopped by to tell her, "Pretty lady, you try too hard. The wood has direction. All you have to do is help it." She wonders if too much advice is clouding her mind.

Luke moves on and stops at Ernesto's bench. The two of them huddle over a sketch.

"What's this box going to be for?" Luke asks.

"Going to give it to my granddaughter," Ernesto answers.

"Is she a woodworker?"

"Oh no, my friend. She is seven years old. It can be for her trousseau."

Ernesto sticks his barrel chest out. Vanessa can't stand it—as if any kid these days has a trousseau. There's a sheen on his forehead that tells her he smells of garlic today. She watches Luke dip his head. "Everybody over here. I want you to see how Ernesto has mitred his corners."

Vanessa sets down the sandpaper—at least they're not being summoned to the altar of Heather this time—she positions herself at the back of the group leaning on the workbench behind her. She's in a comfortable space where she can watch Luke without him seeing her. She isn't aware how intensely she's absorbed into his body, hers swaying gently when he bends to hug the wood as he talks, until she hears him say, "Then you can insert a cloth liner to make the box more of a showpiece." Instantly, she is angry with herself. She's been busy watching again without listening. She's missed the explanation of something she might like to do with her own box.

Too frustrated to begin listening now, she lets her mind wander completely. She is thinking how well Luke wears his work jeans when her thoughts unexpectedly leap to Tom and Lucy. In her mind's eye, she can see the two of them slowly moving down the curve of Park Drive toward Grenadier Pond, a place where Lucy loves to pretend she's a retriever on the hunt. But this time of year the road can be covered in a slick of ice, and the wind can move across Lake Ontario with a ferocity that makes even Lucy hunch into her doggie coat. She imagines the few strands of brown hair Tom has left, the ones he insists on greasing and combing back, are still stuck down. She's watching Tom give Lucy's leash a gentle tug when she hears Luke ask, "What are you going to line it with?"

"Pink velvet," Ernesto says.

Oh my god, what is Ernesto thinking? Vanessa can't help but roll her eyes. When her eyeballs descend from the nether region of her head, she realizes the class is staring at her. Had she made a sound, too? Emitted some exasperated sigh?

"Did you have a question, Vanessa?" Luke asks.

"No. No thanks," she says.

By the sixth week, Lucy has figured out when Vanessa carries the duffel bag of tools to the garage, it means they all get into the car and drive off. Lucy is so energized by the adventure, she leaps like a puppy into the open passenger door to nestle at Vanessa's feet. The three of them are in front of the warehouse where the workshop is held when Vanessa opens the door and Lucy, excited to get to the pond, burns out of the car. She is running down the middle of the icy road, her paws sliding out from under her, when Tom jumps sideways to save her from the garbage truck barreling toward them. Vanessa holds her breath and waits for one of Lucy, Tom, or the truck to stop.

After the truck rumbles by, and Tom is standing safely at the side of the road with Lucy in his arms, Vanessa needs to spend a minute sitting in the car to settle herself.

"You are my hero," she says to Tom and puts her arms around him. He smells nice and being against his chest soothes her some, but her heart is still racing when she walks into the workshop.

Things are different. People are not bent over their benches, instead the man named Joe who works one down from Ernesto is talking. "I live near Kensington Market. Ernesto and I have been best friends since high school, when he first came here from Italy. He didn't speak a word of English then, but we worked together at the same table saw. We learned to communicate through wood."

As Joe finishes, Ernesto hoists his espresso cup and says, "*Salute*, my friend."

Luke swings his eyes around toward Vanessa and says, "Hi there. Heather suggested, since we don't know much about one another, we should each say a little. So what about you?"

Vanessa's immediate thought is, Have I missed Luke's intro? She wills herself to be calm and speaks. "This is my first wood-working class and I'm really enjoying it."

Luke stares at her for a moment until it registers this is all she's going to say. When he moves on, she quietly sets out her glue and clamps, and barely listens to the others, until Luke begins.

"My turn, I guess. Well I live in Slabtown where I've been working alone for a lot of years restoring an old Victorian farm-house. It's the place where I've honed my woodworking skills."

Heather puts up her hand, pink pearl nail polish flashing. "Where do you find the discipline to keep working like that on an old place?"

Luke smiles. "At the risk of butchering what I think some famous opera singer said—it's not discipline, it's devotion. Woodworking is a spiritual thing for me. Almost sacred."

Vanessa looks at her clamps and wonders if she has any discipline. She knows she lacks devotion. Possibly spirituality, too. She's nervous when Luke walks toward her.

"Big day. Putting it all together," he says.

Her hands tremble. He wears his Hart House t-shirt, again. To distract them both from her shaking hands, she asks, "Do you like Hart House?"

"Oh yeah. Do you know it? Such beautiful *cinquefoil* shapes in the trusses."

Vanessa says nothing. She doesn't know what *cinquefoil* means and has to admit she never noticed the trusses when she was a student at the university.

Luke turns and moves toward the front of the class where she thinks he's going to make a group comment. Instead he picks up an L-shaped piece of wood and carries it back to her.

"This is the dovetail joint I showed the class a couple of weeks back. I think you missed seeing it. Maybe next box, you can use this technique on your corners." He sets the shape down on her workbench, so she can see the interlocking pieces of wood at the corner. The pieces look like his tanned and her translucent fingers joined.

"You have to be precise with the cuts," he says. "When you mark your pencil line, a decision needs to be made. Line on, or line off."

"What do you mean?"

"No sitting on the fence with the dovetail. The joint won't fit, if you don't decide in advance whether to cut the pencil line off or leave it on."

"Okay. No sitting on the fence with this."

"You can keep the sample. Study it when the time comes for your next challenge."

Luke leaves his offering and for a moment Vanessa thinks she should return it for fear of what it might represent.

Vanessa is at home in the kitchen feeding raw carrots and apples into the juicer. She likes to stare out the window into the backyard and let her thoughts drift while she listens to the machine masticating. By the time she's adding beets for Tom's blood pressure, she's pondering what Luke's major might have been at university. She settles on Philosophy, deciding this for no reason other than he seems to be a deeply solitary and contemplative person. She's having fun with the carpentry of his character, assembling a truly heroic figure, when Tom walks into the kitchen and disrupts her prince building.

"Looks like there's been a bloody murder in here," he says.

She steps back to see red beet juice flowing down the cupboards and onto the floor.

"Oh god, sorry. The jug shifted and your beet juice is on the floor."

"That's okay," he says. He moves toward the cupboard to get the mop. "I'm not planning on having a stroke tonight."

They are quiet over dinner, and when the dishes are loaded, Tom goes down to the basement to assemble his hunting gear. The next day, he and his buddies are set to go on an overnight to a wetland near Gananoque. It's a place they travel to every year, mostly to drink beer and swap stories, but occasionally to venture into a waterfowl blind and pretend to be duck hunters. Vanessa never liked that they do this, but she knows, especially this year, it's good for Tom to get out. She says nothing and goes into the den to sit at the computer. She stares at the screen for a time before typing 'Slabtown' into Google search.

After some pecking, she finds a map that shows the town near the end of the Beaver Valley Road, where the Beaver River heads away from the Blue Mountains before dumping into Georgian Bay. It looks to be about an hour and a half drive north of Toronto. It's an odd name, she thinks, curious she's never heard of it, but still it must be a decent size if it's a town.

She's about to turn off the computer when she sees a link to a property for sale on Slabtown Road. She decides to take a virtual tour, clicking through the photos until she comes to one that makes her stop. It's a shot taken on a sunny, summer day, and it shows a slab of concrete abutting the river where a mill must have stood. The caption says *a favourite swimming hole*. In the picture there's a distant image of a man poised on the slab ready to dive into the river. The scene looks elegant and timeless.

Later in bed, she lies in the dark and listens to Tom breathe. He's not exactly snoring, it's more of a rhythmic pre-snore, but she knows when he starts out like this that once he's in full REM, the snore will be loud and continuous, and she will not sleep. Before she lets herself get exasperated, she goes downstairs to the divan in the living room and nestles under the duvet she keeps there. She closes her eyes and the image of the man poised at the river is still there, only this time she is up close, and it is Luke. His hand holds hers, their fingers interlock, and the two of them are ready to dive into the river together. She thinks back, how his hand has already steadied hers when his body glided with her along the length of a plank. How but for an inch between them, he could have cupped her, completely enveloped her. She finds the fingers of one hand at the spot on her other hand where he'd first touched her. Restless with the thought of him, and having no urge to curb desires she hasn't felt in too long a time, she can hardly believe her body still works in the way that it does.

After her body is calm again, Lucy comes to lie on the floor beside her. Vanessa drops her hand to stroke the top of her head. "You're such a good doggie, Lucy," she says.

In the morning, Tom's voice wakes her. "Go back to the bed. I'm sorry if I kept you awake. The guys are here. See you tomorrow. Come on, girl."

Lucy picks herself up off the floor. Her paws click across the hardwood toward Tom and the open front door. Vanessa hears the sleeting rain outside, and burrows further into her duvet.

"Be careful," she croaks in a sleepy voice. She's a touch sad thinking about Tom alone in a duck blind in the driving rain.

In the early afternoon, she decides to perk herself up by changing into some nice clothes. She puts her cerise sweater over a lacy camisole, pulls on new slim-leg black pants, and affixes a sterling locket around her neck. She adjusts the chain so the locket's silver heart reflects light up to her face. When she backs the car out of the garage between gusts of wind and sheets of rain, she believes she's only going as far as Bayview Avenue to shop for groceries and treat herself to a cappuccino. But when the sun suddenly comes out, she finds herself following its light along Bayview to Highway 401, then across to the Islington exit where the ramp is infused with gold and beckons her to follow.

At the intersection of Finch, she stops at a donut shop for a coffee. She Googles Slabtown on her phone. It seems further away now, but she's already on the edge of the city so why not keep going. She puts the phone away, looks in the rearview mirror to refresh her lipstick and drives out of the parking lot.

By the time she arrives at Beaver Valley Road, the sky is no longer sunny and an icy wind is coming off Georgian Bay down the valley. As she nears the top of the road, close to the ski resorts, she grips the wheel for fear of sliding. She's all the way to

the t-intersection outside the town of Thornbury before she realizes she must have passed the turnoff.

On the way back, her wipers move so fast in the driving rain
she almost misses, again, the small white sign pointing to
Slabtown. After she makes the turn onto a dippy cement road,
which changes to a rutted, dirt lane as soon as it crosses the river,
she realizes Slabtown is barely a hamlet.

The first house on the right is a lofted cathedral-style structure with a ghostly metal sculpture stalking the front yard. This is
an artisan community, she thinks. She's busy focusing on an
earth-rammed house in the middle of a small meadow to her left,
when the car reminds her she's still driving by taking out a sign
at the turn before the end of the road. She has to sit for a minute
to think what to do. She doesn't want to get out because of the
sheeting rain, but she knows she must. Must at least try to right
the sign.

She stares at the flattened board with *Lucas Parker Cabinet
Maker & Lumber Supplier* painted on it. She holds her pink
umbrella with its sure-release titanium trigger over her head.
When she looks up, she sees the sign is lying in the mud in front
of an old Victorian house, and on the porch stands Luke Parker.

He starts across the yard holding a sweatshirt above his head.

"Hello, Vanessa," he calls.

She watches him pick his feet over the dips of wet grass and
mud. Once he's near, he says, "I knew I'd have an unexpected
visitor when I spotted a black fox in the field this morning. Mind
if I get under?"

Vanessa stares at him blankly. He gestures with his thumb
toward her umbrella.

"Oh, sure. Sorry. Yes get under. And sorry I took out your
sign, Lucas." She is embarrassed. She's used his full name. She'd
been reading the sign instead of looking at him.

When she set out, she had no intention of actually seeing
him, but now that she's here and he is underneath her umbrella,
close enough for a kiss if she felt prepared, she has no clue what
to do. She asks, "What did you take at U of T?"

"What?"

"The Hart House t-shirt."

He looks at his chest to confirm he's not wearing the shirt.

"Okay. Yeah. That shirt. Where did I get it? I think they gave it to me after I finished restoring the bar in the old officer's dining hall."

"But what did you take at the university?"

"Never went to university myself."

Up close, even stripped of his university degree, cocooned under her pink umbrella, Vanessa confronts the bare truth of it. She is falling in love with this man.

"Luke," a woman's voice calls from the direction of the porch, "what are you doing out there?"

"Hey, honey. It's just one of my students. I'll be back in a sec."

The woman's voice continues. "Cranberry scones are getting cold."

"Stick 'em in the oven for a bit, hon."

"Okay."

Luke turns back to Vanessa. "Shauna, my wife," he says. "She teaches culinary arts." Then as if to prove she's good at it, he pats his stomach. "Best fed man in the county."

Vanessa wants to touch his belly too, yet as she thinks this, a wall of reason slams up through the ground and practically hits her with a physical force. He's married. He's happy. He's well-fed. His words in class—*I worked alone for many years*—merely meant *I worked alone*. They did not in any way mean *I am alone*.

She can't help herself, she turns to watch the backside of a curvaceous blonde and a tow-headed toddler disappear through the porch door. For a second, she's not sure she can continue standing so close to Luke. Her face and fingers are tingling with hurt and disappointment.

"Come on into the house and get dried off," Luke says. "Try a scone."

"Oh no thanks, I can't. You're busy with family. But let me help you with your sign."

"Don't worry. I'll fix it tomorrow. Nobody's coming by today anyway. At least come into the shop. Take a look at that Rockwell lathe I've been telling the class about."

He walks back across the yard, and not really wanting to, but not knowing what else to do, Vanessa follows.

As they walk, Luke asks, "What are you doing out here anyway?"

"I was in Meaford and took a wrong turn."

They both know this is nonsense, but he leaves it alone. They move toward a large, restored post and beam shed. It looks as if it might have been a stable for the horse and carriage that belonged with the house a century earlier. Luke pushes on the door and an aromatic puff of warm air escapes from inside.

"That's hazelnut we're smelling. I'm working on a fancy ski cabin over at Devil's Glen. I love burning the leftovers," he says. "And there's the lathe." He points to the corner as he bends to add a piece of wood to the potbelly stove that's beside them.

His space is a dream compared to the cubbyhole Vanessa has set up to work in next to the furnace at home. Each of the large north-facing windows has a view of the forest or the meadow, and there's a hook or a shelf for everything, including the many pieces of intricate gingerbread trim hanging to dry. But what really attracts Vanessa is the tidy mound of fresh sawdust and shavings in the corner of the shop. The mound looks like a nest to her.

"What's the pile for?" she asks.

"I'm building a path for the kids through the brush along the edge of the property. They love travelling through there."

"Aren't they lucky to grow up here. How many kids?"

"Two and one more on the way."

With this information, she is so inexplicably unhappy, she has no thought other than to get away.

"Great space, Luke. But look, I have to get going."

"Really? It's nasty and it's getting dark. You can wait it out here, if you like."

"I'm absolutely sure. I have to be back in Toronto before seven tonight."

"But you barely looked at the lathe."

"It's nice," she says. She doesn't know what words a person is supposed to use when admiring a lathe. "Really. I have to go."

"Okay then. But be careful crossing the cement at the river. It can be slippery when the weather's nasty."

She is so anxious to get going, she triggers the automatic button on her umbrella and gets hung up on the doorframe. She yards on it until one of the spines snaps and the fabric tears.

"Oh, too bad," Luke says.

"No worry. It's a cheap thing."

She scuttles across the yard knowing she looks like a humiliated sparrow with a broken pink wing flapping at its back. How could she be so out of touch with the reality of this man's life? She's a more than middle-aged fool carrying a broken Italian designer umbrella.

The shame of it has her hunched behind the wheel as she drives back down the road. She does not see the cement slab until she's skidding across it toward the far bank of the river. Her car moves sideways and lodges in mud at the edge of the forest. She guns the engine and feels the car dig itself deeper. When she picks up her phone, she sinks even further with the frustration of having no battery left. *Why the hell did I Google the directions to Slabtown so many times?* Impulsively, she crams the remnants of the chocolate donut she'd bought back in Toronto into her mouth. Then she drains the dregs of coffee while she watches the last of the light in the sky disappear.

After a couple of hours sitting in the miserable, howling storm with not a single car passing by, she knows in her bones nobody will be coming or going on such a treacherous night. Her only option is to call on someone who lives in Slabtown to help.

The wind feels like it's going to take off the top of her head when she alights from the car. Within seconds, her umbrella blows inside out and lifts from her hand to lodge in the branches of an overhead oak. The armature hangs just out of reach like a small pink pterodactyl.

As she makes her way past the ghostly steel structure in front of the cathedral house, her coat's lining reaches the saturation point and she feels a wet slick move down her back. Water soaks her cerise sweater and camisole. She hammers on the door of the cathedral, though she knows no one is home.

She is shivering by the time she circles the rammed earth house, and has gone around it three times looking for a door before it dawns on her, it's still under construction and nobody even lives there yet.

She is close to crying when she makes her way up the hill toward Luke's house. She creeps past his battered sign, now sunk in mud, and across the lawn toward the front porch. She stops when she sees inside the brightly lit kitchen. There's a young girl, maybe six years old, sitting beside the toddler she'd seen before. Luke stands at the end of the table. They're all watching Shauna flip a pizza pie crust, laughing and cheering every time she throws it up and catches it. Somehow her successes clinch it for Vanessa. She cannot intrude on this perfect family.

Not knowing what else to do, she edges sideways in front of the window toward the workshop. When she reaches it, she pushes on the door and feels some relief as warm air hits her face. The potbelly stove has a few embers left from Luke's stoking. It's dark though, but for the small glow from the stove, and she has to touch her way around the lathe and the drying racks toward the nest of shavings and sawdust. She peels off her wet coat to leave it on a stool near the fire, and hangs her sweater and camisole on an empty drying rack. She takes down Luke's work coat to wear whiles she shakes off the chill. Under the coat she finds his Hart House t-shirt. She pulls the shirt on, smelling him as the fabric passes over her nostrils.

Bundled into his clothing, she lies on his nest to breathe all of it in.

Vanessa only intended to stay long enough to warm up and give herself time to figure out what to do next. So hours later when the embers die and the cold wakes her, she's alarmed to find she's been in a deep sleep in this intimate space. She takes off Luke's coat and t-shirt. She briefly thinks about stuffing the shirt into her purse, but scolds herself for the thought. She smells it once more before putting his clothes on the hook where she'd found them. She rakes sawdust out of her hair with her fingers. Her own clothes are only slightly damp when she pushes open the door, to check the yard, to make sure no one is there. Then she skirts around the edge of the property and heads down the road toward the car. It's cold and it's dark, but at least the wind and the rain have stopped.

After an hour sitting in her car, she watches the first light of morning come up. Everything seems less daunting, so she tries to back up once more. But the wheels spin uselessly in the mud, and she is out on Slabtown Road starting to walk toward Beaver Valley Road, when she hears a vehicle coming behind her. She turns to see an old red pickup driving down the hill. The truck stops beside her. Shauna and her daughter are inside it. Vanessa feels exposed and vulnerable in front of this woman, knowing she's spent a night wrapped in her husband's clothing sleeping in his sanctuary without permission.

"Need some help?" Shauna asks.

"No, I'm good," Vanessa answers.

"Are you Luke's student from yesterday?"

Vanessa does her best to feign confusion. "Luke? No. I'm waiting here for my husband."

"Are you sure? We can drive you out to the main road."

"No, I'm fine. I like the exercise. He'll be here soon."

Shauna stares at Vanessa as if to say, Who do you think you're kidding? Her daughter looks up at her with an expression that could be one of alarm or annoyance, it's difficult to tell. Eventually, after what feels like a lifetime of awkwardness, Shauna puts the truck in gear and drives off.

While Vanessa stands on the shoulder of Beaver Valley Road, she imagines the conversation Shauna will have later with Luke, how the two of them will try to piece together what might have gone on. She is so desperate to get away, she sticks her thumb out to hitchhike and is grateful when the second car that comes along picks her up and takes her to a garage where there's a tow truck.

The truck has an easy time pulling her car from the muck, but the driver isn't able to dislodge her pink umbrella from the oak tree.

"A marker from your visit." The driver chuckles. Vanessa has to laugh a little, too.

—

Lucy is beyond excited the next week when she sees Vanessa carry the duffel bag of tools toward the car. The day is unusually warm for early December and when they pull up in front of the workshop, Vanessa thinks briefly about walking the park with Tom and Lucy instead of going inside.

"I really don't want to," she says.

"Why?" Tom asks.

"Some of the people are beginning to bug me. I'm glad it's almost over."

"It's the second last one. Go. Have a good time." Tom plants a kiss on her lips, then adds, "Lucy and I will. Won't we old girl."

"Make sure she doesn't kill any ducks," Vanessa says as she gets out of the car.

"Are you kidding? After last week's performance. It's confirmed, the two of us are the worst duck hunters ever."

She is lacklustre in class, worried what Luke must think, what Shauna might have told him. Even more than usual, she avoids talking to anyone. But halfway through, Ernesto starts to go from bench to bench showing off his second box, the one lined in pink velvet. She's nervous about what to say when he gets to her. She has to consciously prepare not to show him she thinks it's creepy how out of touch he is with today's standards, making a chest for his granddaughter's trousseau.

He takes his time, sharing jokes and laughter with people as he goes, until he gets to Joe's bench. There, she hears him tell Joe, "She'll be eight in January, my princess." His eyes are gleaming and he wipes the back of his mouth with his hand as he says, "She's very bad with the leukemia now. I am only hoping my little angel makes it to her birthday." He does not come to Vanessa's bench. He walks to his own, where he sits on his stool and stares at nothing.

She feels guilty and confused by her thoughts. She is becoming a small-minded person and should have known better than to think he was seriously building a box for her trousseau. She slaps on a second coat of varnish without waiting for the first to dry. Ernesto notices and comes over to her quietly. "Excuse me, lady.

I don't mean to interfere, but you should wait until it's dry." He begins to wave his portable hairdryer over her box, helping her to speed the process.

She looks at him, sees the unhappy but friendly eyes, and wants to tell him she's so sorry about his princess, but she knows she wasn't supposed to have heard what he'd said. Besides, she's afraid she'll weep herself. When he shuts off the dryer, he says, "There. You take it home and give it one more good sand before you varnish again."

So it is with all the intention and understanding of grief that she gets into the car after class is finished, and finds a grim-faced Tom.

"What is it?" she asks.

"It's Lucy. She ran off down at the pond. It took me a while to find her and when I did she was in the woods on the far side by the houses, and she couldn't walk very well."

Vanessa turns to look at Lucy in the back seat. She is small and curled into an unnaturally tight position.

"Do you think she pulled something?"

"I don't know."

By the time they're fighting rush hour traffic across town, Lucy is only semi-conscious.

Dr. Purdy, the all-night vet, asks Vanessa and Tom to wait while he takes Lucy into the examination room. When he comes out afterward, he sits in one of the waiting room chairs across from them.

"I think she drank antifreeze," he says.

"How could that happen?" Tom asks.

"Well some guy realizes he hasn't changed his antifreeze in a year, and he takes advantage of this warm spell. He dumps pink liquid down the driveway, goes inside to get more, and along comes Lucy who drinks up what tastes like lemonade to her."

Dr. Purdy folds his hands, lets this much settle in. Then he opens his hands to add, "She's going to die. We should euthanize her. Her kidneys have shut down. I'm sorry."

Vanessa is silent on the way home. How can she blame Tom? He's a good man, he loved Lucy more than she did. He's beating himself up a hundred times more than she is. And she's the bad person in all of this. She's the one who ran away to another man's nest, all Tom had done was take the dog for a walk. Yet somehow she does blame him. But for what? She's not sure.

"Where are you?" Tom asks.

The question startles Vanessa. "What do you mean?"

"You seem a million miles away."

"I don't know. I'm wandering in my mind."

At the next stoplight, Tom puts his hand on top of hers. "It's just you and me now. No wandering. Okay?"

Vanessa tries to smile, but only manages to make a strange half-whimper when she moves her lips.

Luke begins the last class with what sounds like the wrap-up. "You've all done a fine job. It's been a pleasure working with you. I'm no good at goodbyes, so I'll say bye for now. But I'm here to help with finishing touches."

As soon as he stops talking, Vanessa sees Heather start to move from workbench to workbench holding a badly concealed card she's asking people to sign. She slinks lower and lower after each person signs, making it all the more obvious what she's doing. Vanessa is upset by the notion of it. She knows that the *thanks for everything* she'll scrawl at the bottom of the card is a pathetic understatement considering all that has gone on. To make up for it, when Heather asks for a small donation toward the gunsmith-style screwdrivers she's purchased as a parting gift, Vanessa hands her an over-generous $20. And she can't help but ask, "Really? Luke makes guns?"

"No. No," Heather whispers, "they're just very fine tools. They register best in the recesses."

After Heather tiptoes away, Vanessa looks down at her own box. She wants to line it like Ernesto had his. Not in pink velvet, but in white satin. She's mad at herself for not listening when the process was explained, but she'd rather grow roots into the cement she's standing on than will her feet to move forward to ask Luke for help. She slides over to Ernesto.

"I'd like to line my coffin… I mean my box. Can you help me?"

Ernesto lets out a friendly half-bawl of a laugh and says, "My lady, you will not fit in that box."

"Sorry." She laughs at her slip. "It's not my coffin. It's my dog's. She died last week."

"Oh, I'm terrible sorry, lady." It surprises her when he gives her a hug. He smells of ginger soap and toothpaste, not a hint of salami, red wine, garlic or espresso.

"It's Vanessa. Hi, I'm Vanessa," she says. She realizes how ridiculous this is, here it is the last class and she's introducing herself.

"I know, my beautiful lady. You are Vanessa."

Ernesto takes out one of the velvet panels in his box and shows her how it's covered and fitted into the lap edge. By the time he's helped make edges for Vanessa's box, it is fifteen minutes before the end of class. She can see Heather assembling the gift ready for presentation, so she thanks Ernesto and quietly packs up her tools. While Luke's back is turned to help a student at the front, she moves toward the exit. Ernesto follows.

He hands her a business card and whispers. "My son's restaurant. Bring your husband. We can talk about woodworking and I can help you with the lining if you need."

She smiles. "Thank you. Really, thank you for everything. We will come."

She means it.

On the weekend, Tom goes out to the plum tree in the backyard. The warm front has held, and he wears only a cardigan and a light pair of work pants. He clears away the remnants of a few rotted plums they hadn't harvested earlier in the fall. He begins to dig underneath the tree at the spot where Lucy liked to sleep on a hot day. After a few minutes he turns and waves to Vanessa, who is waiting at the kitchen window. She comes and stands beside him.

"Are you sure? You worked hard. It's very nice," Tom says.

Together they look at the pine box that now holds Lucy. It's almost as if from the beginning she had made the box for their beloved furball. They'd told Dr. Purdy a small lie, said they would bury Lucy immediately at Tom's brother's farm in Newmarket, didn't mention they'd be keeping her in the freezer chest so Vanessa would have time to make a satin lining.

Vanessa takes Tom's hand. "Yes, I'm sure. Maybe, I will build another one to put your beautiful tools in. I'll make it sacred this time."

Tom digs one more layer down and they stand for a moment beside the grave.

"We have to work hard to let things go," Tom says.

He lifts the box into the hole and together they drop soil on top of it.

Bastion Square

That morning when a particle of unknown composition skittered under the bedroom bureau, to a place the broom wouldn't reach, Vanessa had to get on her hands and knees and flatten herself like a shore crab. Even when she was as flat as possible, her left arm wouldn't cooperate and stuck up awkwardly as if her exoskeleton were broken. She peered under the bureau and poked blindly with her right hand, coming out with more than she expected—a large ball of dust and hair with multiple unidentifiable bits stuck to it. Tom came into the room while she was on her knees examining the contents—food, insect matter, flakes of human skin? Possibly all three.

She held up the ball. "Where do you think this stuff comes from?" she asked.

"Why don't we hire someone to help with the house?" Tom said.

"I'm serious. You never see this kind of dust floating around in the air. Or out on the street corner. But here, in the bedroom, it's everywhere."

Tom looked at her without speaking, and she was left alone kneeling in the middle of the floor perplexed by the mystery of the ball. When she stood up, she heard the front door close. She moved to the bedroom window to watch Tom walk down the driveway. He wore his light windbreaker, and no hat, even though it was late December and snowflakes swirled around his head. He turned left at the corner and she knew he was headed up to Bayview, probably going for coffee. Unusual that he didn't ask if she wanted to join him. He'd done the same thing the day before. Was this a new habit? To not ask? Did she deserve it? Probably.

Now two hours and an inch of accumulated snow later, she begins to wonder where in fact he has gone. Even Tom can't linger this long over a coffee. She tries to remember what he had on his feet when he left. A search of the front hall cupboard confirms he hadn't worn his galoshes. Perhaps he has gone to the gym and worn his waterproof jogging shoes, but she finds his workout bag in the bedroom cupboard with the shoes inside it and his stained basketball sneakers beside it.

When he returns, he won't tell her where he's been. He says she'll find out soon enough. It isn't healthy they live so much on top of one another that they can track each other's movements down to the precise moment one finds a dust-ball under the bureau, and the other goes for a walk in the snow without a hat, a proper coat or galoshes. It was easier a year back when they still had their dog Lucy. She at least gave their life some shape. No direction home pops into Vanessa's head. Is it a Bob Dylan song? She can hear Bob's young voice singing the words. She calls down to Tom. "No direction home—is that a song?"

"It's a movie," he says.

"Really?"

No answer. She searches it and as usual he is correct. But so is she. Sort of. It comes from the song 'Like a Rolling Stone'.

At the end of the month, on New Year's Eve—they no longer celebrate the season with a tree and a turkey, neither can remember the last time one of them was in a church—Tom brings out a beautifully wrapped gift box. It troubles her. The box is about the same size and shape as the set of wooden chisels he'd bought for her birthday a couple of years back. She has decided she is afraid of the saws and of the feelings she'd developed for the handsome, young woodworking instructor, so there's no chance she will take more classes, but she hasn't told Tom this yet. The thought of it makes her hunch her shoulders and say, "Please no."

Tom chuckles. "That's not how to say thank you."

"Oh. I didn't mean it. I meant thank you." She smiles. It's easier to do that than wade through the layers in her brain toward an explanation of why she's shying away from the gift. She wonders what exactly is in her brain.

The confusion is her problem, not Tom's. And she knows it. Her first reaction to everything lately is dismay and Tom is patient, always trying to make things nice for her. It takes every ounce of self-restraint for her not to tell him she is tired of doing nothing with her life, tired of sitting around and pretending everything they'd done together over twenty-five years of marriage is enough. She knows if she says any of these things it will not only ruin the nice evening he's planned—he's picked up a huge assortment from the deli: black forest ham, sliced beef, salad with arugula and chopped plums, candied ginger, Stilton blue, bing cherries, meringues with pineapple, and handmade drunken chocolates—it will smash their marriage. She doesn't mean to hurt him.

He holds the gift toward her and by the sag of his shoulders she can tell it's heavy. But when she takes it from him, it's so unexpectedly light she almost tosses it in the air. This makes Tom laugh. Vanessa even laughs. A real laugh. He's caught her in the old trick of wrapping something small inside a big box. And he's taken it right down to the detail of his posture. But then she remembers he pulled the same trick on her with an engagement ring years before on a New Year's Eve after she had moved back to Toronto from her foray as a clothing designer in Victoria. Please no, she thinks, not some kind of twenty-five-year anniversary ring.

She is relieved when she opens the box to find it is only two airline tickets to Victoria, leaving on her birthday and returning four days later right after St. Patrick's Day. She really wishes these big event birthdays would just stop. Better to ignore them.

"I thought the weather out west would be okay by then," he says.

She knows she's to blame for his choice of month. She has crowed too often about how they should move to British Columbia, where everything is easier and freer, and the weather never gets colder than a fine spring day in Ontario. It's one of those things she likes to say when she's pissed off on a miserable Toronto winter day. She knows it isn't true, but the weather channel makes her point often enough to make it seem true with its show of early snowdrops, daffodils and grape hyacinths in Victoria's Beacon Hill Park whenever there's a March blizzard in Toronto.

Vanessa begins to help herself to the deli selection. Once she has a few things on her plate, she picks the plums out of the salad.

"Hey that's the expensive stuff." Tom laughs.

"Plums make my teeth feel funny," Vanessa says. She makes a show of rubbing her front tooth. Despite the laugh, Tom looks a little stricken. "Sorry, it's a delicious salad," she says. "I like the pecorino cheese on it. Thank you again." She means it, she does appreciate the effort and she finally lets her shoulders down from around her ears so she can enjoy the rest of the evening.

She starts to tease him about their trip, telling him she hopes he has booked a penthouse suite at the Empress. Tom won't tell her where they're going to stay. He says it's a surprise, a place he's looking forward to seeing again. He's been to Victoria only once, early in their marriage, when he headed west to a conference for school administrators. She's forgotten where he stayed, but remembers he talked about a water view, so it must have been somewhere on the Inner Harbour. Maybe it really will be the Empress Hotel. How grand would that be? Wherever it is, it will be an easy walk to high tea of crustless watercress and smoked salmon sandwiches in the Empress lounge. Possibly even dinner in the Bengal Room with the tiger skins on the wall and the waiters in Nehru jackets serving exotic curries and cocktails.

In the last week of January, Vanessa pulls out her design portfolio and begins to rework a few dress patterns. She wants to modernize her line and is pleased when she manages to introduce a hint of Belgian enigma Martin Margiela's sensibility into her sketches. It excites her to show the structure of the design on the outside with exposed stitching and bits of interfacing. The controlled chaos in her redesign feels like a tasteful unleashing of her creativity. She's chosen an earthy grey and peridot green for the palette because it hints at sprouting spring buds.

She draws a few breaths of hope looking at the reworked designs and for the time being she feels like she's back in the slipstream of things.

She knows the dress shop Amadea where she had worked in Victoria closed some years back, but she thinks she might take her reworked fashions into to the high-end dress shop that shared space with the designer furniture store Delbuccis on Pandora Street. Maybe, she can get some commission work from the shop, or possibly something more steady. She is ready to move forward. This is what she and Tom need. They could start fresh in Victoria and it will be a better life for both of them. They'll live on a street lined with cherry blossoms in spring, and their yard will be a meadow filled with lilies and Garry Oaks, and have an expansive view of the ocean. Perhaps she'll only work part-time and they could even move to the beautiful countryside of Metchosin. She feels so excited by the possibilities, she pours herself a glass of wine and decides to take Tom out for dinner.

A week before they're scheduled to leave, she searches for Delbuccis on the computer. Nothing comes up. Perhaps the store has moved. Or is she misremembering its name? But it's an institution among the wealthy Oak Bay crowd so it must still be going strong somewhere. She closes her computer telling herself once she's on the ground, she'll be able to find it. Truth is, she is afraid to poke further. Afraid to pop the dream she has concocted for their future life.

At the Victoria airport, Vanessa and Tom climb into the back of an overwarm cab that smells of pine car freshener. Tom gives the driver an address on Gorge Road. Vanessa nearly corrects him, to say, Do you mean Government Street?, but then second-guesses herself thinking maybe Gorge Road goes further toward the Inner Harbour than she remembered.

It's all she can do to suppress a groan when they pull up at a Days Inn on Gorge Road in uptown Victoria, a good five kilometers from the Harbour. The motel's design is faux Baroque with domes and sculptural masses that look like party hats. It's lit up like a mini Parliament Buildings with hundreds of little glass bulbs. Some gleaming. Some burnt out. Any view it has is of the gorge, not the ocean.

As the cab pulls away, the sun finishes setting and the wind picks up across the tiny expanse of water in front of them.

Vanessa shivers. Believing her own blarney, she's worn only a light spring jacket.

She follows Tom into the motel's muted grey and steely blue reception area. A bouquet of paper flowers sits on the counter by the empty front desk. Tom rings the bell and when a young woman comes out from somewhere behind, she wipes at her mouth and chews the last of whatever supper she's been eating.

"How can I help you folks?" she asks. The smell of French fries wafts from behind the counter.

In the room, Vanessa puts her suitcase on the luggage rack and suggests Tom put his in the bathtub. "Keep it off the ground," she says, "in case of bed bugs."

"Do you not like this room?" Tom asks. He draws back the brocade drapes. "Look a beautiful view of the water."

"It's dark. We'll see it in the morning."

"Come on. There's nothing wrong with this room."

Tom wheels his luggage into the bathroom and closes the door behind himself without waiting to hear if she has anything more to say. When he comes back out, he says, "You're right. It's not as nice a hotel as I remembered. Still there's a great little jerk chicken place near here. We had a lot of fun there. You and I can, too."

"Who is *we*?" Vanessa snaps. She is remembering the blonde principal from North York that Tom talked about too much after he returned from the conference. Vanessa met her only once. A large, coarse woman, tough in that *I want to dominate you way*. Necessary perhaps for a woman to be a successful high school principal back then, but surprising Tom would befriend someone like her. Why is the room evoking old hurts she hasn't thought about in years? Or is it just that another year has passed?

"Doreen," she spontaneously blurts.

"What about her?" Tom asks.

"Is she who you ate jerk chicken with?"

"Yeah. Sure. Doreen and a bunch of other people. It was years ago. Let's not go there, Va-ness-a."

Whenever Tom articulates every syllable in her name, it means he's running out of patience. She knows she needs to pull back or risk setting the entire holiday on edge. Don't make waves, an expression her mother used when she was a child comes to mind. She lets the waves in the room float out over the gorge.

"Okay, sweetie," she says, "let's go find some jerk chicken."

They walk out the front door of the Inn and Tom looks up and down the street before deciding to turn in a direction that takes them further up the gorge.

"I thought I would see it from here," he says as they walk.

"I don't want to wander aimlessly for too long," Vanessa says. "I hate to admit it, but I was wrong. Victoria can be really chilly in March."

"Is that right, little girl," Tom says.

She likes the gentle bear hug that comes with the expression, but after a couple more blocks with nothing resembling a commercial shop or restaurant, only houses that look warm and inviting, she turns and says, "Let's go back."

"Okay. I don't think the restaurant is here anymore."

She can tell Tom is disappointed, and she is disappointed for him but too cold to keep walking. He is making the popping sound with his lips that he makes when he's confused. Back at the front desk, he asks, "Is there a jerk chicken place around here?"

"Jerk?" the young woman says.

"Yeah. Jerk chicken."

"There's a KFC not far. Or if you're looking for decent food close by, the Ramada next block over has Heckler's. It's also a comedy bar. It's fun."

At the back of the Ramada and downstairs, they find Heckler's Bar & Grill. The round tables are covered in chocolate brown vinyl. A mic and a stool stand in the centre of the room. The crowd is young and most of them look like they've had a few cocktails already. Tom heads for the empty table right beside the stool and sits down.

"Good view from here," he says.

Vanessa stands beside him. Tom looks up at her. "Do you not want to sit at this table?"

"It's fine," she says and sits down. Why didn't she tell him she would be more comfortable not so close to all the action? Not so centre shot in front of all these young people? Is this her way of being nice to Tom by letting him take control? She vows not to make him pay for it later. To stick with her choice and not sulk. Still, this is not how she imagined celebrating her birthday.

Tom picks up the triangle standup specials menu on the table. "Looks like we're going to get chicken after all. Fifty flavours of wings. Sleeves of beer and Caesars for five bucks. Not bad."

"I know you're disappointed," Vanessa says. "It's fun to go back to places you enjoyed in the past. I have some places I want to see, too."

"What?" Tom says. He is busy trying to get a waiter's attention. When the callow young man comes over, Tom orders a sleeve of beer and twenty wings. "Ten with honey sauce and ten with ranch dressing."

The waiter looks at Vanessa.

"Do you have a full menu?" she asks.

"Yeah. You want something to drink?"

"A Caesar, please."

The drinks come. The Caesar in a heavily salted glass tankard with a stick of pepperoni plunked in it. No menu.

Tom's wings come. Still no menu.

"What else do you have besides wings?" Vanessa asks the waiter.

"Steak's on special. You need to order quickly. The show's about to start."

"Okay. Steak. Medium rare." She knows he didn't hear the last part as he'd already turned to walk away. But she isn't going to complain, even if the steak comes tough as brokeback mountain. She is not going to make a mess of this night.

The spotlight hits the stool, and a voice over the loudspeaker introduces the evening's opener. "Let's give him a big welcome. It's his second time on our stage since he graduated from high school, which took a few tries, so he's been here lots. You all know him—Mario Spencer." The voice laughs as Mario moves from a table of rowdy drinkers who look as if they are still in high school. They hoot like they're cheering on the local football team. When Mario gets to the mic, he takes off his ski jacket and places it over the stool carefully. He touches it once as if to make sure the jacket is all right with where he's placed it.

"This is all I have left to wear," he says, pointing to the jacket. "Yeah, sad isn't it. The girlfriend and I were at a wedding last week, you know the whole happy couple thing, over to their place afterward for a toast, and some finger food. I fucking hate finger food—way too many bones." Mario stops to let people laugh and only Tom does. Vanessa would have except she doesn't get the joke until after Mario begins to talk again. "After a few drinks I started to think I'd be okay with getting married. You know, as a concept. A hypothesis only. Next morning in the haze of a really bad cocktail flu, I mean a real rager, I stupidly said, 'That was okay.' I was talking about the free bar, not the fifty years of marriage that comes afterwards. But the girlfriend, she thought I was proposing. Right away, she's all about our place. On about how, 'We gotta clean up this mess. We can't have people over after the wedding to see this.' I said, 'What? What *this*?' and she started hurling stuff at me. 'Man,' I had to tell her, 'You're the one making a mess. All my underwear used to be sorted into clean and dirty piles. Now it's underwear everywhere—skid marks touching clean gonch.' She looked at me and shrieked. 'This place stinks like hot garbage. And it's because of you.' Now I ask, is that the way a loving wife is supposed to talk?"

Mario pauses to let the crowd laugh. Tom laughs, again. Vanessa puts her head down into her tankard.

"Turned out that was sort of sweet compared to what came next. She screamed and threw the biggest, dirtiest, skid-marked gonch out the front door. They might have been dirty but they were my best pair. The ones with the beer mugs on them—no seriously, beautiful cotton boxers, high thread count—so I ran out onto the lawn to get them and she locked the door! And here I am with just this ski jacket she so kindly hurled down to me from the upstairs window. I threw the dirty gonch right back at her and she caught them between her tits like the Major Leaguer she is. You know, I might be able to marry that girl after all. But it's going to be a lot work. How about you, sir?"

Without looking, Vanessa knows Mario is talking to Tom.

"You folks married, or just here on a dirty weekend?"

"Both," Tom answers.

He gets a bigger laugh than Mario has so far. Vanessa has to laugh too, but plunges her face into her drink when the spotlight hits Tom. The pepperoni pokes her in the eye. Then somehow when she pulls her face out of the drink she manages to get a heavily salted barnacle from the rim of the glass stuck on the bridge of her nose.

"Oh look, Princess Bride has sullied her makeup." Mario pauses long enough for the spotlight to swing to Vanessa, then he says, "Your bride get shitfaced at the wedding too, sir?"

Tom laughs. His face is open and clear, and he looks like he's enjoying himself. He nods. "Like you said Mario, 'Marriage is a lot of work'."

Vanessa knows he's using his high school principal technique. Repeating the person's name to show interest. He probably has a mnemonic going in his mind, too. Something like *Mario's girlfriend has a pairio.*

Mario closes one eye. He looks at Vanessa through the other eye and makes a pinching motion in front of it. "I'm crushing you, Princess Bride," he says as he squeezes his fingers together. She feels crushed and a bit shaken by the time his set is over.

She barely listens to the main act. On the way out she notices the Heckler's house rules and wonders if they could work for a life.

1. Be nice
2. Shut the f—k up during the show.

"That was a lark," Tom says. "Happy Birthday, little girl. We'll celebrate in style tomorrow night."

Back in the room, Vanessa lies wide awake in the bed. The mattress is too hard. The radiator ticks and the air is dry and dusty. She goes into the bathroom to get a drink of water and when she comes back out, Tom is sound asleep, snoring on his side. She lies down and stares at the mound beside her that is his bare back. He looks innocent and comfortable. She wants to cuddle into the curve of him, tell him she loves him. But she can't, not with real meaning. She'd give anything to have her old, comfortable life back. When they were both working, both productive. The balance between them had been right then. Not working has exposed shaky ground for her. Tom is so much better at entertaining himself; she wishes she could learn from him. She can't contemplate making a break, yet she knows in an odd way her failure to do it is what's killing her. How would she make it on her own? So many things make her nervous since she retired. No, since she was forced out. That is the truth of it, she'd been forced out of her job. She'd ridden the wave of newly retired for the first couple of years, believing if only she and Tom could do something grand like pick up and move west, her disappointment would resolve. Now that they're here, and it is not nirvana, what had been a small tear in her veneer is an open-mouthed gape. The last thought she has before falling asleep is that the vacation has already been spoiled, and she is the spoiler.

In the morning, now that her birthday is well and truly past, she wakes with a resolve to un-spoil the holiday no matter the cost. Maybe things will go well with her portfolio and she will be able to stitch the gaping hole shut. She and Tom go down to the coffee shop for the complimentary breakfast, a sugary Danish and weak coffee.

"If I rolled this Danish up in a ball, the diameter would be less than an inch," she says.

"Like this?" Tom rolls his pastry into a shape smaller than a marble and pops it in his mouth. "Less calories this way."

"Do you think?" She sips her coffee then says, "I'd like the morning to myself to explore some of the fashion shops."

Tom looks surprised. "I thought we'd do that together."

"What do you want with ladies fashion?" she asks.

"You're right, but can it wait a day? Let's do this first day together. Maybe we can see if the Empress has a room for the rest of the weekend."

She doesn't want to wait until Saturday to go into the shops. She knows it's the busiest day and also the day owners are most likely not to be in at all. But a vision of vulnerable sleeping Tom comes to her and she relents.

"What would you like to do?" she asks. She says nothing about a room at the Empress. The thought of the two of them in an over-expensive luxurious space doesn't fit anymore.

"Maybe whale watching," he says.

She shivers for about the twentieth time already that morning, but says nothing because she wants this to be Tom's day. Relief surges through her when the clerk at the front desk says it's won't be good whale watching until May. He suggests they take a bus tour to Butchart Gardens. "One leaves in an hour," he says.

It turns out to be too early in the season for good garden viewing too, but the gift shop is nice. She buys some floral napkins and a box of notecards she knows she won't use even before she's paid for them. At least she and Tom are on neutral territory. Both of them are pleasantly bored.

Early afternoon the next day, Vanessa and Tom take a cab into downtown Victoria. She gets out at Pandora Street and he carries on to the Museum. They will meet later at the Empress. She walks Pandora with her portfolio under her arm. It's true Delbuccis is no longer there and nobody at any of the neighbouring shops can even recall it, or the high-end fashion shop it shared space with. She wanders Yates, Johnson, and View Streets and finds little she recognizes. She treats herself to a peanut cluster in the chocolate store, and the woman who runs the shop tells her she's been downtown for a lot of years and she can't remember a Delbuccis.

"Why don't you check out the Smoking Lily, over on Government Street," the woman says. "They design their own clothing and they've been around for longer than me."

Vanessa walks into Smoking Lily feeling confident. She is on her home turf now. She takes a browse through the racks and thinks the fashions look solid, but could do with a touch more sophistication. Something she can bring to it. She asks the young clerk for the sales manager.

A woman in her forties, her hair tied back in a loose ballerina bun, comes out from the back of the store.

"Hi. I like your shop," Vanessa says. "I was wondering if you know whether Delbuccis is still operating somewhere in Victoria?"

"No they closed a long time ago."

"Oh too bad. I was going to show them my designs. I've worked in fashion for years in Toronto."

The manager says nothing. Vanessa reminds herself people in the west can be aloof—perhaps mention of Toronto was not smart—but she plows ahead. As soon as she puts her portfolio on the counter, she wishes she hadn't. The woman says, "All our pattern drafting is done in-house."

What had she been thinking? She knows better. For some stupid reason she'd thought Victoria had remained frozen in time. It's inappropriate for her to cold call with her designs. She herself would not have given a designer the time of day if one had simply dropped in on her, even when she was a young sales manager just starting out at Creeds. Her lips feel numb, but she continues to flip pages and hears herself saying, "The palette evokes the gaiety of spring buds." Jesus, who is she now? Some sort of noblewoman from the Hapsburg Court? It's as if she's gone tone deaf on everything. Why hadn't she researched where she was going with this?

The manager says, "The designs are interesting but we're looking for more practical styles without hanging threads and such."

"And such?" Vanessa repeats.

"Thank you for bringing your work in. Perhaps you could try up island. There's an interesting turnabout shop in Duncan."

The bell on the shop's door tinkles as it closes. A turnabout shop? A retread for tired, old clothing. Vanessa feels like throwing her portfolio in the first trashcan she comes across on the street. Why had she been so careless with her own career? Everything she ever does is always so tightly planned, this has been a huge misstep. Then in a wild mood swing, she tucks the portfolio tightly under her arm with love, and hurries down Government Street toward the Empress Hotel. By the time the hotel is in sight, she's hugging the portfolio to her chest, telling it and herself everything is okay. Exposed stitches are not hanging threads, they're an homage to structure. When she is in front of the hotel, she is telling herself she's not a bad person, she can still make things happen. She does wonder, though, when and how she'd gotten so out of touch. Or had she been lazy, hoping everything had stayed free and simple in Victoria like it was when she was in her twenties?

It is too soon to meet with Tom for tea. She doesn't care. She can waste time looking in the lobby shops and she has no energy to go anywhere else right now.

What she thought was the main door to the Empress seems to be permanently closed. She finds the new entrance off to the side of the grand building, but she's disoriented in the remodeled, less majestic lobby. She has to ask the concierge where high tea is held. He points to his left and says, "In the lounge. Enjoy."

The lounge too has been modernized—no more of the gilt Louis the 14th chairs she liked. Tom is already there, against the wall in a leggy cane chair that barely seems to support him, but is probably better than him fussing in a too-small Sun King piece of gilt furniture.

"I came early," he says. "It was too cold to walk further along the Harbour. I forgot how much crap there is on the sea-wall past the Parliament Buildings."

Vanessa is hurt by his insult of what she believes is the prettiest walk in Victoria. "Why? What was along there?"

"A wax museum and some gifty sorts of places." He lowers his voice almost to a whisper. "The tea is $75 a person in here. Sheesh."

She is disappointed there'll be no smoked salmon and watercress sandwiches—it wouldn't be worth it if Tom is going to grouse about the cost—but she needs something to steady herself. "Perhaps we could have a glass of wine here, then check out the Bengal Room."

"Closed," Tom says. "Too colonial for this day and age, I guess."

"Oh no. What's in there now?"

"A bar that looks like a spaceship. It's more comfortable here. Let's get that glass of wine and decide what next."

After several glasses of Cabernet Sauvignon—it would have been cheaper if they'd ordered a bottle—Vanessa asks the waiter, "Where do you suggest for dinner? Somewhere not in the hotel."

"Il Terrazzo's my favourite," he says. "It's over on Johnson Street. Not far."

The restaurant is in an old town courtyard with several attractive and warming brick fireplaces. "Not too close to any fire," Tom says to the hostess. She takes them to a corner table under a cubist painting of a woman. Vanessa asks Tom if she can sit looking out into the restaurant. She knows she's too discombobulated to eat her dinner and stare at a pulled-apart woman painted in broad strokes of vibrant yellow, green and red. But the pizza and the wine are good, and after they dip their way through a shared tiramisu, she says, "I know a great club. Harpo's. Good music, especially on the weekends. It's close. In Bastion Square."

Vanessa lets out an exasperated sound as they climb the stairs off Wharf Street toward the club entrance.

"What?" Tom asks.

"Harpo's isn't here anymore. It looks like it's called the Upstairs Cabaret now."

A sign outside the club with an emoji of a tripping dude painted on it says *DJ Lanky ShankZ tonight*. Below it a smaller sign advertises *Green Beer*. "Of course it's St. Patrick's Day," Vanessa says. She pulls open the door and is met with a wall of sound a younger person would recognize as music. She is momentarily blinded by a profusion of spinning purple lights, but makes her way toward where she remembers there are bar seats. Once her eyes adjust, she sees the interior is roughly the same, although there is hardly anyone in the room yet. It always used to be packed.

"What can I get you folks?" the bartender asks.

"Scotch," Tom says. "Bar scotch is good."

Vanessa looks at him "Really?" she says. "Okay, me too."

An hour and two scotches later she is sloppy in her seat. The club is filling with noisy Millennials. A lot of the girls have hair the colour of cotton candy: pink, blue, apple green. And the boys have manbuns and beards. A few of each sex sport bleached blonde hair with profuse black roots. Everybody is taking shots of something green, hooting and making the woo noise. Vanessa sees Mario from Heckler's with his arm around a quiet looking girl with mousy brown hair. They're sticking their tongues out for a selfie. Mario's tongue seems to be coated with cream. Only a few in the room are dancing, the odd purple flash of light catches an undulating rear end or a flying arm. But Vanessa is beginning to enjoy the music. An interesting combination of beats with shimmering sounds that make her want to move her feet. Lanky ShankZ is discoey without being too disco. He's having fun, his headphones hanging off one ear, dancing to his own music. She wonders what the move he's making back and forth like the *cut* motion in front of his throat is called.

She makes the cut motion in front of her own throat and Tom laughs. She moves in to yell at him, "Want to dance?" and to her surprise, he jumps up and onto the floor. He is well-coordinated for such a big man and she decides to watch instead of joining in.

Lanky ShankZ slows things down and Tom begins an almost Druid-style ballet, which makes Vanessa start to contemplate why she'd dragged him to the site of a disastrous heartbreak for her from so many years back? The bass player, Jake, the man with whom she'd fallen madly in love when she lived in Victoria, dumped her in this club, when it was still called Harpo's, for a younger, sexier, more talented woman. There is a certain bookend quality to her sitting now in possibly the exact same seat as she had been when Jake began the dump, one that she followed backstage to the green room in her inexperienced state of how the romantic crushing of a heart proceeds. Was it that crushing which made her such a devotee of safe? Did she forever after damn herself to do the safe thing? Or had it started earlier? Had there been a slow clipping of her wings starting way back?

As she sips at what she vows will be her final scotch, her mood of disordered mush begins to coalesce into a hardened, cracked mud. She realizes she got herself drunk on purpose, and with the realization she lands on something from even earlier in her life. Something she'd almost forgotten, that had to do with Tom. Not as her lover. But Tom as a fellow teacher, senior to her, back in Ontario, before she went to fashion school. When she had been in training for her teacher's certificate.

A colossal waste of time that had been, her training to be a teacher. Tom's unknowing (*was it?*) interference with her and her obsession with the student in the grade thirteen English class she'd been teaching. How Tom had held the door of the dance hall open to her when she'd followed the student from the grad-uation party she was supposed to be chaperoning into the parking lot. "Watch yourself," Tom had said. That was all it took to shake her back to reality and understand how wrong it looked for her to have followed the student. But oh the results of her not tailing him had been so terrible.

Vanessa in that moment full to overflowing with a deadly concoction of scotch and wine is convinced Tom ruined her life that night. He's the one who permanently hooded her potential romantic, freewheeling nature. He made her as boring and mousy as Mario's fiancé. She had no *joie* left in her after Tom's interference. All the characters in this drunken play of hers swirl in front of her like the lights on the dance floor.

Tom comes off the floor and motions it's time to go. Vanessa slips from her bar stool. On the way out of the club, she looks over at Mario again. He is surrounded by a small crowd of people listening to him shout above the music's roar. His girlfriend is alone leaning against a brass rail drinking a green beer. Vanessa sincerely hopes the girl will not become Mario's wife.

The club door bangs shut behind Tom and Vanessa. A fog hangs in Bastion Square and Vanessa briefly wonders if they paid their tab. As quickly as she thinks they have probably skipped, she doesn't care, and she turns toward Tom.

"I'm tired of your face," she says. It startles her. She hadn't intended to say it, but now that it's said, she isn't going to take it back either.

Tom makes the popping sound with his mouth and his eyes blink twice. He lingers beside her for too long considering what she's just said. He tilts his head toward hers, and moves his mouth into a half-smile as if he is savouring something good trapped inside himself and isn't going to share. By the time the two of them walk toward a cab at the curb his face has that same unfiltered, open look he'd had at Hecklers. She wonders if a person is truly open whether that means they can extend themselves forever. Their vitality and optimism never dwindles, and life becomes a series of boundless larks.

They say nothing to each other on the way back to the motel. As she follows him into Days Inn he looks really tall to her, like he used to when he joined the high school boys in the gym to lay up a few baskets. He was handsome dribbling down the school basketball court in his business suit toward the hoop's skirtlike net. He dunked the ball more often than not. It surprised Vanessa whenever she saw how good a player he was. It surprises her now to see that once she is no longer on safe ground and in her mind he is a free agent, how much more attractive it makes him.

GLADIOLA ISLAND

Vanessa watches her silly, square hybrid rental car rock between a decaying Econoline van and a dilapidated grey Toyota with spirit catchers hanging from every fastener. The van is so old it could have been on the last BC ferry she sailed thirty years ago.

She is headed for what should be an island paradise at the top of the Georgia Strait. But she can only focus on whether it's going to be the murderer's van or the hippie's spirit car that scratches her rental. She breathes in. Breathes out. Tries to be mindful. Looks to the horizon for balance. For a moment all she can see is ocean rolling up to meet the sky. It should have liberated her.

The trip seemed like a good idea, when she'd ducked into the organic grocers to wait out the pissing spring rainstorm and spotted a stack of 2018 Laurel Bush Centre catalogues beside the fresh raspberries. What could be better than a writers' retreat on Gladiola Island in the middle of August?

But as the weeks ticked down, and the Toronto weather improved, worries about her choice started to mount. *What if people think my writing is worse than Hallmark? (What if I think some of Hallmark's cards are clever?) What if my room is unsleepable? Worse, what if I forget something essential?*—even the catalogue warns 'no stores on the island'.

The sight of the looming island makes her queasy, so she stops looking out and walks the decks instead. There's something a little off about the crowd. Some are just island folk, straw hats and mismatched wool socks give them away. And a few are vacationing families: a boy, a girl, a mom, a dad and various combinations. A lot, like more than half, are couples, around her age, middle-aged or so, and mostly well heeled. This is remarkable.

Men don't go to writing workshops, especially not with their wives. When Vanessa finally spots another woman who seems to be on her own, she slows her pace to ask, "Are you headed to Laurel Bush?"

"Yes," the woman practically gushes, "for Sharing the Heart Trail. And you? Are you here with your hubby?"

Vanessa staggers a bit with the shift of the ferry, or perhaps it's the woman's response. Is she going to be navigating a horde of exploring couples at the Centre? She would never have signed up if she'd known. Especially since the split with Tom has not gone totally smoothly.

She ekes out a weak smile. "No. I'm going for a writing workshop."

"Oh," says the woman. "I didn't know they ran other courses this week."

"Me either."

Then for no reason Vanessa can fathom, the woman pushes her sunglasses up her nose and says, "You'll do fine."

The true gravity of the situation does not sink in until the lithe little man at reception, the one who looks as if he could yoga himself into a pretzel, tells her, "There's unlimited herbal infusion and caffeine-free rooibos."

"And wine at dinner?" Vanessa asks.

Pretzel man makes a squishy sound with his mouth before answering. "We seek an unobstructed experience for our guests."

A voice in her head screams, "You expect me to navigate this without Cabernet?" She turns to see if she might find a different answer elsewhere in the room, and her knot of disappointment lands on the smiling, preppy couple registering in the line next to hers. They are fussing with multiples of Louis Vuitton luggage while being checked into an ocean front suite with private hot tub. So it hurts doubly when yoga pretzel man tells her, "Madam, you will be in the A-frame with shared facilities and a forest view."

"Ommmmmm," she chants as she drags her luggage toward the shack in the woods, the guest cart too full with Louis Vuitton to accommodate her. She's so absorbed in the task of getting to her cabin, she doesn't notice the majestic cedars, the wind eddying high in the branches, the lower boughs reaching down like welcoming arms. The only thing that keeps her going is the calming rhythm of the ocean behind her. She's just starting to relax about being there, when she arrives at her shack.

It's dismal. Nothing but two A-shaped squats joined in the middle by a bathroom. It needs paint and the walls shake when she unlocks her door. The bed in the room fills the entire space, and she has to use the Ommmmmm resonance in her throat to manoeuver around it, to get to the communal hall and shared bathroom. Once there, the bathroom door bangs shut and the walls shake, again. In a small fury of need, she unpacks her toiletries, covering most of the convenient shelf and counter space, and as she does, she makes up her mind that no matter how quiet the people in the adjoining squat turn out to be, she will hate them forever if they wake her even once with a dropped tube of toothpaste or an over-enthusiastic midnight pee. She is as certain about this as she is that no quantity of herbal infusion or caffeine-free rooibos will be able to touch the situation.

When she exits the bathroom, she walks to the end of the hall and peeks behind the door which is open into her cabin mate's side of the structure. A purple, crushed velvet dress is draped over a suitcase abandoned in the middle of the floor—its contents a jumble of different coloured velvet dresses and sensible sandals. Good, it's not a wandering couple, she thinks.

The first time Vanessa smiles is at the communal dinner table when Sandy, a fifty-something-year-old dressed in a Lacoste golf shirt and surfer jams, picks up his registration material and reads aloud the description of Sharing the Heart Trail. He stops after the words *to learn the spiritual and inner connectedness that will lead to deeper emotional and physical commitment.* He says, "Oh god, Lisbeth, you had us drive all the way from Southern California for this? It sounds like so much bullshit."

"Thank you for that." Vanessa laughs.

Lisbeth, who is so anorexically-thin her floor length tie-dye t-shirt and silver hoop earrings look like they might drag her into the depths of the earth, pushes a piece of kale around her plate and asks, "Thank you for what?"

"Sandy's honesty," Vanessa answers.

Lisbeth is clearly displeased, and makes no response other than to swoop up her and Sandy's plates. Vanessa watches as she glides over the beautiful strawberry-blonde fir floor toward the cleanup bins, where she begins the process—food scraps into the slop, napkins to recycling, cutlery separated from the plates, each dipped into a tub of ginger-scented water.

"Well, enjoy your evening session," Sandy says as he stands to follow Lisbeth. When he moves from the table, Vanessa hears a sound like, "Grrrrump." She can't tell if it's directed at her, but suspects it might be.

After she clears and sorts her own dishes, she shuffles shoeless across the floor to the rack of cubbyholes where footwear is stored during meals. She shoves her feet into her running shoes and starts up the wood chip path to Cedar House for the first meeting of her writers' group. The ice in her glass of lemon infusion tinkles when yoga pretzel man from reception stops her.

"Please, no glassware outside the dining hall. We provide hot and cold thermal mugs for sale in the gift shop."

"Okay. I'll remember for next time," she says, and carries on up the path with glass in hand.

The group seated at the long table inside Cedar House is only ten, a better size than the mass of couples. The leader who sits at the head of the table, and whose catalogue picture resembled the Maharishi, turns out in real life to look more like an Anglican minister. As if by secret code no one talks, waiting for the minister to decide when. A full five minutes after the start time, and his lips begin to move.

"Greetings. My name is Nigel. I'll be the leader for your Profound Writing." He pauses to let the profoundness of what he's about to say be silently announced. "You're all trying to vanish into your work, when what you really need is to find the space to do it in. Before we introduce ourselves, I want to begin with a simple, silent affirmation: *I can do this. I am ready.* Close your eyes and feel it in your core."

The curly-haired young man to Vanessa's left, one of two men in the group—a surprise there are two—repeats the affirmation loudly. "I CAN do this. I AM ready."

Nigel peers down the centre of the table. "Silently," he says. "Try to stay in the trance of creativity."

Vanessa can't make the affirmation at all. Instead she is thinking, I can't do this, I'm not in the mood. She looks across the table at the round woman in her late sixties, probably ten years older than she. The woman is wearing the purple, crushed velvet dress that had been draped over the suitcase in the other squat adjoined to her cabin. She seems sort of folded in half, almost asleep. Vanessa wonders what she is thinking.

When the trance of creativity has stretched almost to the snapping point, Nigel asks everyone to say "just a little" about their writing. Most are vague, say things like *have been writing for a long time, started in high school, picked it up again recently.* Crushed velvet cabin mate turns out to be named Kathy and is "into poetry".

Vanessa is relieved there appear to be only two pros in the group. One is a pretty lifestyle reporter for CTV named Jill. Nigel diagnoses her as needing to "shatter her seriousness". And the other is a strong-boned, first-time novelist named Barbara who doubts she can write a second novel. Nigel tells Barbara to "find the fun in the writing again".

After Vanessa introduces herself, mumbling something about hoping to write a decent poem one day, Nigel's one-second diagnosis for her is to "get over your disappointment". She doesn't remember saying anything about being disappointed, but there it is, pronounced in such a way she knows she's not supposed to argue.

Nigel ends the evening with, "Let meaning trump mood. You do not need to be in the right mood to write. And everybody please listen for the barred owl on the way back to your cabin. He's the one hooting, 'Who-Cooks-For-You?'"

She follows the tiny beam of her flashlight down the path toward the A-frame. She keeps some distance behind Kathy.

She's not ready to introduce herself, and she's feeling guilty about spreading her stuff around the bathroom, especially after Kathy told the group she's recovering from some unspecified illness and needs writing to "find herself again". Nigel told her to "coddle the fragile egg".

Vanessa wakes in the middle of the night and hears the barred owl's hoot. She feels a touch sad her answer is nobody.

At breakfast, Vanessa finds an empty table in the corner away from the windows. Most of the couples are clambering for seats with ocean views, and she can't locate any of the writers in the sea of faces. She is content to sit on her own, but halfway through her bowl of granola and hemp hearts, a couple of women with matching haircuts, matching hairbands, matching glasses—in fact, matching everything except one is in a wheelchair and has an assist dog—begin to make their way toward the table. She is unsure how to assimilate this information and keeps her eye on her bowl, but soon feels the dog by her feet, and hears the sound of a chair being moved away so the wheelchair can pull up.

"Hi. I'm Donna, and this is my partner Sarah. The dog is Megabyte. Mind if we join you?"

"Not at all," Vanessa says as she puts her hand down to pat Megabyte, who promptly licks her fingers making it impossible for her to continue eating with that hand.

"Are you here with a partner?" Donna asks.

"No, I'm here for a writers' course."

"Oh how great. I've always wanted to be a writer," Sarah says. "What have you published that I might have read?"

This feels like the most personal and defeating question that could have been put to her, and for a millisecond Vanessa is tempted to ask, "And what bed-death experience are you here to work out?" Instead she smiles and says, "I'm a beginning writer."

Everyone looks uncomfortable with her answer and, as soon as she can without being rude, she rises from her chair. "Got lots to do. See you later." She moves toward the sanitation station, and then to the drink station to fill her expensive, new thermal mug with rooibos.

Most in her group are already gathered at Cedar House by the time she sits down. Nigel has not yet arrived, but Kathy her cabin mate, who wears dark green, crushed velvet this morning, speaks up.

"Is anybody else finding this place irritating? Someone on the other side of my cabin snores and visits the washroom all night long."

Vanessa tips her head down and is glad she hasn't yet introduced herself. She'd tried not to pee so often during the night, but she'd drunk too much herbal infusion hoping it might make some sort of happy substitute. And although toward the end of their marriage Tom had begun to mention she snored, she never really believed it until this very second.

Only the curly-haired young man, whose name Vanessa has already forgotten, engages Kathy. "You better change rooms," he says.

"Who is changing rooms?" Nigel asks as he enters from the ocean-side deck. "What an incredible view we have out here."

"I am," says Kathy. "I'll be back right after I arrange it with reception."

Kathy gathers up her multiple notebooks, her colour-coded pens, her laptop, and exits.

As soon as she's out of earshot, Nigel says, "I wonder if she's coming back?"

No one responds, so Nigel continues. "Well if she doesn't, keep in mind she was here for a reason. Possibly to give one of us a lesson. Okay, today's headline is *choose and commit*. I want you to reflect on this. If you've already chosen what you're going to write this week, go do it now. If you're having trouble, write a synopsis of two or three things, then commit to one. Go for thirty minutes."

People scatter. Vanessa walks with her empty notebook to the far end of the yard. She sits in a plastic chair and stares into a tangle of blackberry bushes just coming ripe. This is bogus, she thinks. I've spent a thousand dollars to have someone utter less than a hundred words per hour, while I sit in a place less comfortable than my own home and still don't write. She can hear the woman named Alicia somewhere behind her talking non-stop. When she turns to find out to whom she's speaking, she sees Alicia is alone at the picnic table and appears to be talking to her computer.

Vanessa pulls out her iPhone to check the time, but starts checking and rechecking emails, as if commanding one more search is going to turn up something more interesting than a renewal notice from an online magazine she never subscribed to, or another proposition from Svetlana who thinks she's a lonely old man. After fifteen minutes have passed and nothing new has appeared on her screen, she begins to scribble in her journal. She writes a title 'Under the Bell Jar'. It's to be a poem about her marriage. The only other words she writes on that page are *trapped from the beginning.*

She flips to another page and writes a new title 'Spring Breakup'. Almost immediately a number of lines come to her. *Every year it's a surprise when the ice goes out/ the year father went down/ up to his waist/ we laughed/ the crack/ the fish floating belly up/ it was nothing/ everyone survived/ except the fish/ until the year the water split/ split at the seam/ and he drowned/ the wild iris blooming/ at the edge of the stream that fed the breakup/ we won't pick the iris/ ever again.* She looks at the page and thinks there may be something here. But where did it come from? Her father never drowned.

Still, she feels excited. She's got something she wants to try out on the group. See what they think of the nub of her new poem.

"Time," Nigel calls from the deck.

Once everyone is assembled back in the room, he asks, "What did you learn about your writing?"

Alicia pushes a button on her computer and it talks, reciting words to the group in an Alicia-cyber-altered-voice.

"Stop," Nigel says. "What is that?"

"It's Dragon Maker," she says. "Voice activated software."

"Okay. On your own time, Alicia. We're not here to workshop people's writing. We're here to explore the writing experience itself."

This is news to Vanessa. She thought it was a writing work-shop, and she's not the only one who's confused. When Nigel asks again, "What did you learn?" Jill the CTV reporter says, "I'm writing a memoir about traveling and depression, and I'd like to share a few lines about my family…"

"Stop," Nigel says. "We are here to learn about the process of writing, not to hear what you are in fact writing."

Only the curly-haired young man seems to get it. He puts his hand up and when Nigel nods, he says, "I learned writing can be meditative if you trust. I free wrote without critiquing on two different myths, and when I finished I realized only one was worth committing to."

"Thank you, Stephen," Nigel says. "A writer's biggest chal-lenge is to *choose and commit*. The next story not yet written, is always more sparkly than the one which you've put serious words on the page for."

Nigel doesn't ask what any of us learned, instead he says, "Okay. Back out to write some more. If you haven't committed that's your challenge. If you have, then go deeper. Go for forty-five minutes."

By the time Vanessa is walking back for the morning wrap-up, she's beginning to understand what Nigel has been telling them. She did go deeper with 'Spring Breakup' and now it's a mess; she actively has to resist moving back to 'Under the Bell Jar'. It looks so much more sparkly with only four words scrib-bled under the title. The struggle to commit is tiring.

At lunch Vanessa carries a tray with organic leek soup and beet salad to the end of one of two quaint wooden tables nestled under the apple tree outside the dining hall. She cannot face the hall right now, and the tree is like a beacon calling *sanctuary* to her. Seated at the other table are a young Asian couple and an older bearded man whose facial hair looks like it's knit to his face. The beard looks up at Vanessa and says, "We're in deep session right now."

"Excuse me?" Vanessa answers.

"I should explain," he says. "I am one of the counselors with the couples' group and we are in session here."

Vanessa's mind screams. *I paid my money. Just because these people messed up their marriage doesn't mean you all get to take the prime eating spot. My marriage screwed up, too.*

All she says is a simple, "Okay."

Knit-beard looks at her. "Thank you for understanding. My name is Joshua. Perhaps we'll meet again under lighter circumstances. Embrace your afternoon."

The young bride, who has been making utterances like an injured bird throughout Joshua's sweetness and light banishment speech, lets out a sad "so sorry" when Vanessa picks up her tray to move on.

She walks toward the dining hall. At the door, she passes Alicia, who is embracing a young woman adorned in crystals. She hears Alicia say, "Thank you for letting me share the adventure of my life." Vanessa imagines what the words would sound like in a Dragon-cyber-voice.

By the time she finally sets her tray down in the dining room, the soup has scummed over. She picks at the beets and fennel on her plate. Two beets slip over the edge of the plate and onto her clean linen pants before flopping to the ground. To distract herself from the unappetizing mess she's created, she decides to join the dessert line. The line is long, but the sight of lemon pie at the end picks up her spirits, that is, until the chubby older woman ahead of her motions for her husband to come forward. "Morris. Morris. Get up here. We'll be late for the afternoon if you don't budge in."

Morris's look announces he'll be in for it if he doesn't do as commanded. He slips in front of Vanessa, a sheepish grin on his face. This endears him to her so she asks, "How's it going in your group?"

"Oh, it's all very interesting," he says.

"Do you have to be part of a couple to join?"

"Yes. But some of them are not doing so well. Some are…" Morris lowers his voice as if he's sharing a secret "… some are even the same sex."

"Morris!" his wife thumps his chest. "Not doing well and same sex are not synonymous."

"I know, sweetheart. I'm just saying." Chagrined, he turns away from Vanessa for the remainder of their inch-forward toward dessert.

She leaves the dessert table feeling jilted, her slice of lemon pie jiggling.

"The headline this afternoon is *use only words that serve you.* What do I mean by this?" Nigel asks rhetorically, but RainDear, the red-headed organic farmer from Belleville doesn't catch the drift. She starts to answer.

"I'll share an anecdote of something I learned during light therapy about the power of full spectrum to reinforce the body's service."

"I'd love to hear about that." Alicia encourages.

"No, let's not pursue this," Nigel says, "otherwise we'll spend all our time on it. What I want you to keep in mind this afternoon is that even if your mind tells you *this is a mess*, it's your job to love it. Your words to yourself should be *this writing is meaningful to me.* And if you have not committed yet, to commit is your foremost job. Now go, write for forty-five and come back committed."

Vanessa heads for her chair at the back of the yard, but is beat out by Alicia who is already there setting up Dragon central. She's tempted to find another chair and pull it nearby so she can sit and stare into the blackberries, until she hears Dragon repeating back, "The horse throbs wildly under my thighs."

No wonder Nigel doesn't want us to share, she thinks.

She settles at the edge of the deck and stares out into the ocean until she feels compelled to scribble a few more desolate words in her journal about the spring breakup. After a time the lines she writes blur into breakups in general. The line she loves the most—*the moon hangs like a bruised plum in the sky/how dare he do this to me*—doesn't fit into either of the poems she's started. They're not wedded to anything. Besides she's the one who left Tom, so maybe these words belong to a poem about another breakup.

"Writing tools down," Nigel calls.

Vanessa is close to crying when she sits back at the table. She hadn't expected so many thoughts about breakups to surface at the workshop.

Nigel begins. "Realize that whenever anyone finds out you are a writer, the next question will be, 'What are you writing about?' Shut that one down as quickly as possible. It will suck the life out of you if you talk too much about your writing. And really, nobody cares. Why is that? It's because most people believe they're going to be writers too, and they want to pick your brains."

Curly-haired Stephen holds his hand high to speak. "But is it okay for us to say we are writers?"

"Of course it is," Nigel says. "That's why you're all here, isn't it? To go deeper. To say a simple 'I am a writer' will serve you well. Relax, man. Arms at your side."

Stephen grins and puts his hand down.

"Okay," Nigel says, "we'll go around the room and all of you give a one-liner as to what you're writing about, then I'll say, 'Tell me more' and you give me your exit line from the conversation."

Nigel starts with Stephen, which means Vanessa will be asked last. She likes this until she realizes as they go around all the good shutdown lines are disappearing. She especially likes the novelist Barbara's line, "I don't want to talk about it too much, it will let the air out of the tires." And the weaver Trixie's line, "I'm too superstitious to talk about it, the prince of darkness might be listening."

By the time Nigel gets to Vanessa, her heart is pounding and her mind is almost blank. She stammers, "I'm not really sure what I'm writing. I've started a bunch of poems that are running together and nothing is jelling."

"Hmmm," Nigel says. "Tell me more."

"Well, I hope you'll get to read one of my poems someday."

Nigel looks at her with lips moving like a lizard in advance of his words, then finally he says, "Sounds kind of snarky."

Vanessa is stunned. He'd responded to all the others with positive words, or with nothing at all but an encouraging smile.

Her dry run was the lone one to have garnered a big thumbs down. She's left completely unclear how *snarky* fits with the philosophy of using only words that will serve her well.

Her heart hammers in her ears and she is conscious that her face is turning purple with hormonal stress. For the rest of the afternoon, she doesn't hear most of what Nigel has to say until she becomes aware everyone else is packing up. She follows on autopilot to the door, and is about to exit when Nigel says, "It's apparent to me, Vanessa, that you have not yet committed. This evening it is your task to commit." He pronounces the last word with a great flourishing point at her, like his is the finger of God.

The naked painter on the beach helps Vanessa find wine on the island. She had not realized she'd wandered off the Laurel Bush property and was in front of private land until the man popped up from between two logs with a canvas in his hand and a streak of navy paint on his upper thigh.

"Ahoy," he says. "Can I help you?"

"I was out for a walk, didn't realize you were here."

"No, of course you wouldn't. Are you from the Bush?"

"You mean Laurel Bush?"

"Yeah. Their property ends a few hundred feet back, but lots of folks end up here."

"Oh, I thought they owned the whole point."

"No. They just behave like they do. The property stops at the laurel hedge."

"I don't even know what laurel looks like."

"It's that shiny green leaf bush you see at the edge of their property. Not much to look at really. Sort of a weed if you ask me. But how are you enjoying it?"

Vanessa is having trouble juggling the conversation while maintaining appropriate eye contact. The man who is about her age is obviously an accomplished nudist. He carries on his side of the chat as if there's nothing unusual about his appearance. Her gaze keeps drifting around his surprisingly fit anatomy, from right nipple to left, down centre hairline to navel, then on to occasional collision with scrotum and attachment, and back up to navel.

She wishes she had worn sunglasses because she knows her eye-balls are popping. She hears herself answer. "It's okay but I'm dying for some wine. They should have told us there was no alcohol on the island."

The man laughs. "You need to come to the Spa."

"Excuse me?"

"Regulars at the Bush know all about it. Come with me."

He crooks his finger as he heads down an overgrown trail leading from the beach toward a ramshackle cottage. She feels vulnerable following him, but she keeps saying to herself, com-mit, commit. When they get to the porch he turns to ask, "What do you want, honey? Smokes, pot or alcohol?"

"I get it. Spa. Clever. Do you have any cabernet?"

"No, honey. Only white table wine this week. It goes good with the homegrown. Can sell you some wine plus a couple of joints for thirty bucks—this week's special."

"I haven't smoked pot in years ..."

"Well time you did again." He laughs.

Vanessa stares. She knows she needs to respond and not knowing how to be around the offer of pot, but knowing she would really like the wine, she says, "Sure I'll take the special, but I'll need somebody to share the pot with. I don't really remember how to do it."

"That's a good deal for me. I'll spark one up with you, honey."

He fusses with the pillows on one of the cedar porch chairs. He points to the chair and says, "Take a load off."

Vanessa is uncomfortable with the notion of sitting down, because it means she's staying for a while, but once seated, she realizes it's better than standing because she can face away from his nether region and not appear to be rude. She wonders why she is so uncomfortable, it's not as if she hasn't been around naked men before. He disappears inside.

When he returns with joints and a lighter along with a carton of white wine, she notices a tiny diamond stud glinting in one ear. She doesn't know what to make of it. It's sort of compelling, but sleazy at the same time. Possibly it means he's gay. Though that thought is disappointing. All his enthusiastic smiles and honey endearments might just be friendly affectations.

He puts the wine at her feet, sits in the other chair, lights the joint, and hands it to her. Predictably, she coughs out the first toke before it's halfway down her windpipe.

"Easy, sister." He laughs. "Try that again with a little less enthusiasm."

She manages to keep the next couple of tokes down, but by the time the joint comes by a fourth time, a fearful-paranoid-dead-head feeling has descended. It reminds her why she gave up smoking years earlier, when she moved back to Toronto after her hippie time living in Victoria.

"That's it for me," she says.

"Okay. I'll put this puppy out." He jumps to his feet. "Wrap the rest in foil for you."

She trembles with paranoia as she waves her hand no, but he's not paying attention. He disappears inside and is back in a flash with the pot in a piece of foil that looks like a crushed minnow. Her feet have to get moving and there's no time to argue about it, so she shoves the small dead fish into her pocket, picks up the wine and races down the path toward the beach.

"Quicker to take the road out front, sister," he calls. "Come visit anytime."

Back on the compound, stinking of pot and carrying a box of wine, Vanessa runs into yoga pretzel man from reception. His words *we seek an unobstructed experience for our guests* float in her mind. She giggles. It's inappropriate, but at least it signals she's on to the part of smoking pot that she likes, the part where paranoia is replaced with a sense that everything is grandly amusing.

"Good evening, madam," pretzel man says.

"It is," she answers, hoisting the wine toward him before continuing her sideways drift toward the A-frame. Once there, she flings open the door and glides into the common hall toward the bathroom in search of a drinking vessel. At the end of the hall, she notices the door to Kathy's room is wide open, again. The room is vacant and made-up, ready for the next guest.

Vanessa is definitely on the pot roller coaster now because she suddenly feels a bit down. Kathy never did return to the workshop, and Vanessa starts to believe she had been there to teach her not to be selfish, to be more forgiving, to stop analyzing people. In short to learn to fit in. *Oh god. I'm not fitting in. I'm the only one that Nigel thinks is snarky. But I'm horny and I want to have sex with _____ hmmm, what's his name? the nude painter.*

This last thought stops the roller coaster. The car she's sitting in shudders at the notion of having sex and the fact her mind slotted the naked artist into the blank seems crazy at first. Why hadn't she figured that out when she was staring at the real thing? All of that flesh. How much more obvious does it need to get?

The car swings with the momentum of the roller coaster starting up again, and for a second it turns to the ecstatic when she focuses on having the entire space to herself. She does a grateful fairy twirl in the hall outside the bathroom, then closes the door to the other side, feeling exposed as if in fact somebody has already checked into the room, and she just isn't seeing them.

She sits on her bed and takes the sanitary wrap from the plastic glass. Fitting, she's about to drink heavily fortified wine from a shatterproof container.

After a second glass, she thinks the roller coaster might be slowing down as she drifts into happy memories of being a twenty-five-year-old living in Victoria, a young fashion designer dating fishermen and loggers. But then at the edge of the memory is one that eventually lurches everything to a stop, gives her a clear view of the disaster that was Jake—the bass player who carried a quiver of instruments and the musty smell of sex everywhere he went. The way he'd ended things with her at the club. Heartbreaking. But evidently thoughts of Jake can still settle inside her and make everything stand at attention.

Was it that upending that sent her headlong into a rebound marriage with Tom too soon after she returned to Toronto? Why when she saw Tom lounging at Sunnyside Beach that day had she sought him out to remind him they'd met before?—when she was a student teacher and he was the popular phys ed teacher.

Did she want him to understand what she had been trying to do with that student? That it was honourable. Or was it that Tom was sexy then and she felt like some company?

She gulps a third glass of wine. It helps her to slam the door on the roller coaster, and feel sufficiently girded to tackle the communal dining experience.

Vanessa carries a tray of organic Bengali dinner to the arm of a vacant Adirondack chair at the end of the deck. Joshua the knit-beard is seated at the table beside the chair in deep session, again. He's talking with an over-tall, over-married man sitting next to a pretty but sullen wife. The wife keeps swiping the end of her nose with the sleeve of her sweater.

Vanessa has had enough wine not to care that she is eaves-dropping, and Joshua seems to have given up on the privacy thing. She hears Joshua say, "We all get overwhelmed sometimes. One minute my wife is a nagging princess, the next she's a god-dess. I wait for the goddess moments."

"I do, too," over-tall says. "I wait for them, but those moments aren't coming clear to me. To be honest, we aren't get-ting much out of this workshop. Are their any toolboxes we can take home with us?"

At this, Vanessa turns away out of respect for the awkward young man. But she can still hear everything.

"There are no toolboxes," Joshua says. "Work on one thing at a time. That's the best advice I can give." He stands ready to leave, then perhaps recognizing he needs to do a bit of public relations, he adds, "Watching you two work on the exercises this morning was beautiful."

After Joshua moves toward another couple, the pretty rabbit-nose wife asks over-tall, "What do you take from that?"

"To make conversations just conversations, nothing more. To diffuse. To not feed the fire."

After a minute of silence, a minute when even Vanessa can't swallow her food, they stand to depart. Vanessa sneaks another look. The wife glowers, her embers are clearly waiting to be fed. Vanessa aligns with her, and yet does not want to be her. She feels sorry for over-tall, and half-inclined to jump up, and warn him—She's going to leave you.

Alone on the deck, she feels sorry for Tom. She'd been that angry wife toward the end. She'd infused everything with hostile silence. He'd tried at least to douse her irritated fire. She could have worked herself into a sentimental, overwrought state except that Nigel sits down beside her at the table where over-tall had been sitting, and shows her a bowl of cardamom rice pudding.

"This is good," he says. "My second."

"I haven't had dessert yet."

She is pleased they might have a real conversation about something other than writing, until, out of the corner of her eye, she sees a flush-faced man whose nose looks like it's going to consume his face move toward them. When he gets to the table, he plunks himself across from Nigel.

"I hear you're the leader of the writing group. I'd love to join the group next year. But I'm here with *the wife* this time."

"Yes," Nigel says.

She senses Nigel is getting ready to shut down a conversation that seems headed toward writing. So far, the man is undaunted by the initial monosyllabic answer. She waits for Nigel's exit line.

"What do you talk about in the group?" the man asks.

"Writing," Nigel says. "Tell me about your writing."

Bingo. It works. The man completely abandons his questions and starts with what Vanessa knows is going to be a very long tale that begins with, "Well I have quite a unique story. After I lost my license to practice medicine, I descended into the bottle for a time, but I resurfaced to find…"

As she picks up her tray, Nigel interrupts the man to speak to her. "Have a good evening, Vanessa. Don't forget to work on committing."

Next morning, Vanessa is exhausted. All night she kept waking with dry mouth, not from the wine—although that didn't help—but from too many disturbed dreams about unachieved sexual experiences in which both Jake with his standup bass and the naked artist featured prominently. She knows it's symbolic of her inability to commit, and lies irritated with the thought of it when she hears the morning triangle ring outside the dining hall. While she dresses, she wonders whether the sound of the triangle makes anybody else resonate with an association to the TV show 'Bonanza'—it seems so incongruous with the otherwise new-ageness of Laurel Bush.

In the dining hall, she waits at the tea stand behind red-head-ed RainDear from the writing group. RainDear is engaged in a hug with a plump woman who is not in the group, the two of them embracing, eyes closed, hands moving slowly and lovingly in small circles up and down each others backs. They end with a wrap-up tussle and a satisfied *emmhhh,* followed by another vaguely sexual sound. Then as soon as they appear to be finished, they go at it, again. Vanessa realizes she must have been staring because when they finally do finish, RainDear asks, "Want an omega hug, Vanessa?"

"Oh no thanks. I just woke up."

"Okay. Celebrate your day then."

Vanessa fills her thermal mug with rooibos and heads toward Cedar House. She can't face steel cut oat pancakes after hearing her day is to be celebrated. Especially not with a hangover.

Alone in the yard she pulls out her journal and stares at it. She's written nothing but chicken scratch and dog's breakfast since arriving. It's hard to commit to either one, especially when most of the others in the group seem to have already finished half a man-uscript of publishable quality. She's wondering, What's wrong with me? when Nigel calls, "Everybody. Come on in."

He begins the morning session with, "We all need to get over our own personalities. They get in the way of writing. If you let your personality intrude, even if you block a week off to come away to a retreat, you won't write. You will end up having an affair instead."

"Not if you come on the same week as the couples," young Stephen quips.

Everyone laughs and Vanessa waits for Nigel to shut it down. She's surprised when he lets Alicia tell an over-long story about her penchant for home decorating, which they all hope will somehow end in tale of an affair, but ends with her saying, "I think my obsession with candles is a good example of what you mean about personality getting in the way of writing."

Then Nigel, perhaps out of a sense of fairness, goes around the room and asks everyone what it is they think gets in the way of their writing. The excuses range from the banal— *taking care of the dog, the baby, the garden*—to the strikingly unusual from the quiet, bald man, who issues a showstopper when he says, "My obsession with guns."

Even Nigel doesn't know what to say except, "Still waters run deep, brother."

When it's Vanessa's turn, she's flustered and wants to say to the quiet bald man, Get away. Instead she says, "I don't know. But something's stopping me. I haven't really written anything all week."

Nigel looks at her. "You know what's stopping you."

"Inability to commit?"

"And that's because…"

"I'm afraid."

She surprises herself. She never admits to fear. Never, ever.

"Of what?" Nigel asks. "You don't have to tell us. But think about it. What are you afraid of?"

Vanessa stares at Nigel. She hopes her expression looks impassive, but from the inside of her skull she knows there's a rapid succession of blinks going on. They are commands to self to not cry.

"Now everybody go," Nigel says. "Put your personalities aside and write acutely for an hour and a half. We'll meet back here right before lunch and see what progress has been made."

Vanessa sits in the yard and writes the word FEAR in the middle of the page. She draws a box around it and stares at it for half an hour. Then she writes the word FRAUD underneath it. Even Beethoven could get his difficult personality out of the way to write beautiful symphonies. Why can't she for one second let it flow?

She can't stand how stuck she feels.

—

Something is different about the couples at lunch. A lot more of them are holding hands. Vanessa wonders if this is for show, whether each couple afraid to look weaker than the other holds hands in a show of coupledom—or has some miracle been worked on the group? Even the young Asian bride, who had fluttered like a bird when Vanessa interrupted her counseling session under the apple tree, is sitting happily with her husband who keeps his arm around her shoulder. Only the over-tall, over-married man with the pretty wife and her twitching rabbit nose look unhappy. He holds her purse while she pokes at her *chile relleno*.

Midway through the meal, Joshua the knit-beard rises to introduce his wife Paula, who has a microphone in her hand.

"We've had an incredible morning," Paula says. "Everybody has worked hard beginning with an anger management session where we yelled and yelled, to get all the aggression out. And now everybody feels so much better. Right?"

All the couples, except for over-married and rabbit nose, clap and cheer. Megabyte barks from under a table somewhere.

"Oh yes," Paula says, "who can forget Megabyte? He got the most upset with all the yelling and showed us dogs are less inured to anger than people. But after our anger, we healed through dance. So Joshua, Megabyte and I want to invite everybody at Laurel Bush to join us in a celebration circle of healing dance."

Stevie Wonder's 'You Are the Sunshine of My Life', a song Vanessa had liked up until then, begins to play. Megabyte is first out. He circles the wheelchair in time to Stevie while the others flood the floor. Vanessa follows over-tall and his wife out of the dining room. She walks three paces ahead of him. He still carries her purse.

In the glare of the sun, Vanessa's not sure what to do with herself except to get the hell away from the dining hall. The upcoming afternoon is meant to be unstructured, so she can dive into her writing. Really push it. But since there's nothing to push she wanders generally in the direction of the gift shop. She is leafing through the Laurel Bush cookbook searching for the ginger sesame recipe when Sandy, who drove from South California with Lisbeth, glides into the shop. He has doffed his surfer jams and Lacoste shirt in favour of a hemp manskirt and Birkenstocks. He heads toward the far bookcase, and stops under the sign *Sexuality and Relationships*. He has that same ecstatic look on his face that most of the couples have, so he too has drunk the Kool-Aid. For several minutes, he is intently buried in a book with a red and gold binding. When he's finished, he shoves the book back into its space with a slight self-satisfied grunt, then glides back out of the shop.

Vanessa waits a minute to be sure he won't return. She strolls over to pluck the red and gold book with the title 'Rapture' from the shelf, and opens it randomly. Although it's hard to describe what she is looking at, the words *full throbbing penis* come to mind. She thumbs through several pages until she spontaneously snaps the book shut after lighting on the page that illustrates the proper way to insert Ben Wa balls into a vagina. She leaves the shop with images in her head of Sandy in full battle attire, dangling Ben Wa balls from his fingertips, and follows her feet back to the A-frame, where she unwraps the shatterproof glass in the bathroom and pours out the remainder of the wine.

Vanessa wakes the morning of the last full day of workshop and bypasses breakfast all together. She can see a large number of couples on the porch of the dining room looking too much like they're waiting out a set break at a dance hall. Instead of venturing near, she goes around the building and tries to sneak through the kitchen in an attempt to access rooibos from the rear.

Yoga pretzel man catches her. "Madam this area is private. Can I assist?"

"Yes. You can. You can find me some coffee."

"Brewed coffee is for sale every morning until 10 in the gift shop, Madam."

"Really? How come no one told me this before? This place is messed up."

She is surprised how happy this snap makes her feel. Even pretzel man's wan, beatific smile doesn't take the pleasure away from it.

When she arrives at the gift shop, she snatches the red and gold 'Rapture' from the bookshelf and pushes it toward the young clerk, who is dressed in the sheerest of sheer cotton dresses. She says, "Plus a large coffee to go please."

"Okay. Cream?"

"No thanks, black."

The young woman gives her another beatific smile, as if to say, I hope you find the same enlightened path I'm on without stimulants. But no matter, the coffee is soon coursing through Vanessa's veins, picking up her day as she walks toward Cedar House.

Nigel begins the morning session with, "Fear makes us fuck up. Apocalyptic thinking is ancient, resurgent and wrong. Things are generally better than we believe and we must access our innate joy to really write down what it is we have to say."

He stands at the head of the table in sermon position, while Vanessa sips coffee. She feels her heart palpitate when he raises his hands above the group, his gesture so like a blessing. "Today we will banish fear and find the ritual that works for each of us."

She thinks she's found the ritual. Coffee. But when she's staring down the bottom of her cup, she hasn't had enough. She excuses herself and rises from the table to rush back down the path to the gift shop before the last of it disappears for the day. She orders four cups. "For the group," she says, and scuttles back to the A-frame where she leaves three behind for later. She slips back into the workshop in time to hear Nigel say, "To banish the fear you need to courageously notice what's going on. Sometimes it's just that kick the shit out of yourself feeling that helps you find a courageous affirmation to carry on."

"Flip the magnet," Jill says.

Everyone nods gravely.

Vanessa knows she's missed some important attraction-repulsion metaphor while out scrounging for coffee. She's formulating a question when Nigel interrupts her thought with, "Rituals. What we're hunting down here, Vanessa, is a ritual that will help keep us going. Each of you take a sheet of paper and quickly write on it one *should not*. Then we'll read it and rip it up. Go."

Vanessa is unsure why this has to be done with such urgency and is anxious about all that she has missed while out of the room, including what exactly a *should not* is. But she knows an inquiry is not going to be well received, so she scribbles a few words on a tiny piece of paper and puts it in front of herself with her hand over it. Nigel looks down at her hand but speaks to Barbara.

"You had some big doubts when we started, Barbara, about your ability to write another novel. I sense you have a considerable *should not*."

Barbara smiles and reads from her paper. "I should not have quit writing to put Glen through architecture school, and then once he was finished, I should not have let the bastard stay in the house."

"Bravo," Nigel says. "The start of a novel!"

And on it goes around the table—*I should not have let my family talk me out of being the wonderful writer I know I am, I should not have had so many sexual distractions, I should not have remained celibate for so long, I should not have wasted so much time seeking attention.*

When it comes to Vanessa, she takes her hand off the paper and has to pick it up to read it because the script is so small. "I should not think I am too old to start writing."

"Well done, everyone," Nigel says. "Now rip those suckers up and throw the paper into the air."

Stephen's is folded into a paper jet that he launches around the room. Jill looks so pretty throwing her pieces, it makes Trixie say, "It's like a wedding." But Vanessa's paper is so small there is no ceremony to shredding it. Instead the piece turns into tiny balls that look like something a gerbil shredded. They fall through her fingers onto the table. And worse, when the ritual is over, she still feels old. She scoops up the dirty little balls and crams them into her pocket.

"All right, each of you needs to keep the ritual going. Find the one that works best for you and commit to it. If necessary find a series of ritualistic steps to blow up your anxiety." Nigel looks directly at Vanessa as he says these last words. He locks eyes with her and continues. "But for now, more writing. Go forth and proliferate. That includes you too, Vanessa."

She stews in the chair at the back of the yard. She can't stand that not only is she blocked from writing, she's even blocked from having an effective ritual. She picks one of the balls of ritual paper from her pocket and launches it across the yard with her forefinger. It lodges in the blackberry tangle. She hopes it's the one with the word *old* written on it and a Douglas squirrel will find it and bring it back to its nest where a litter of babies is being reared. What's old becomes young again, she thinks. She writes those words down and thinks about the remains of the joint wrapped in the foil in her room. A remnant from when I was young? she wonders. Maybe pot will help quell the panic she's feeling. There is only the afternoon and the next morning left for her to write something meaningful, and it looks like nothing is going to come together.

Vanessa flips to the page in her journal where she'd begun to write 'Spring Breakup'. She runs the pen through the title and changes it to 'Marriage Breakup'. A few new words creep onto the page.

> Brilliant sunshine caught us under
> the bell jar of our honeymoon,
> anxiously examining our nuptial parts—
> mandibles, shamefuls, wings and hearts.
>
> So soon his sails unfurled, his rigging squared,
> he flew across the lake,
> while I waited on sandy shore,
> a collector's pin in hand.
>
> Frozen I remained. Still every year
> it's a surprise when the ice goes out,
> the fish floats up, a sign the seam has split—split at the seam.
> The collector's pin, firm in hand.

She looks at the poem. It's beginning to take shape, although she doesn't like the look of the uneven lines, and she changes the title back to 'Spring Breakup'. After all she and Tom had split in spring. She remembers the day after they returned from the short vacation to Victoria. She moved into their comfortable den and made a cave for herself until they could figure out who was going to live where. The sun was shining and the last of the snow was melting, the first crocuses bloomed in the window box outside the den. But what's with the line *pin in hand*? She can feel it now, a genome of ancestral experience tingling at a small spot on the end of her thumb and forefinger. Waiting to do something. But what?

The couples arrive to lunch in a ball of pulsing energy. They're readying for their final night rave in the woods. Although Vanessa is jealous of their exhilaration—she's in line behind a couple who breathlessly make plans to collect feathers after lunch for headdresses—she's also relieved she won't have to do anything tribal. She's about to mention bird mites to the couple, when Joshua and Paula slide in front of her with the ease of entitlement that comes from being the leaders of the biggest tribe.

The two of them enthusiastically go through a playlist for the evening's music. Vanessa overhears Hebrew wedding dance, Kenyan dance loop, First Nation's remix of 'Good Ship Lollipop', and Sister Sledge's 'We Are Family'. At the mention of Sister Sledge, her mind drifts to the fringed couture halter-top she'd bought years ago in Yorkville and had thrown into her luggage at the last minute before coming away. Maybe she should put it on, for the fun of it. This is the point Nigel is trying in his overly ministerial, psychoanalytical way to get across. To have fun with writing. With life itself perhaps.

Lunch is polenta spears with Kalamata olives on romaine lettuce fresh from the Laurel Bush garden, together with as much wheat-free, green goddess dressing as Vanessa can scoop onto her plate. She loves the dressing and is gobbling it up when she decides even though she's not invited to the rave, she'll dress for a party later anyway. She can dance alone in the A-frame to the strains of music that will filter through the woods from the sound system she'd seen being dollied through the trees that morning.

By contrast to thoughts of a rave, the afternoon workshop is dull. Nigel asks everyone to think about the one thing they will come away with, to record this thing in a ceremonial way, and to be ready to keep it in a place of prominence. He dismisses them for an hour to ponder this one thing and create an artifact that reflects it. The length of time surprises Vanessa. Nigel seems to want some deep thoughts on this issue. Or maybe he's running out of steam, in which case she's pissed off.

When they reassemble, Trixie has made a small weaving with a finger loom that stitches out the words *I will pray*. Stephen has carved *Keep on Writing* into a block of wood. Julie, who also turns out to be a dancer, performs a short piece she calls *Juicy Artist* that she asks Barbara to video for her. The creepy bald guy who never talks has a blank piece of driftwood that he says will be his tablet of ever-changing creative visions—it looks like a gun to Vanessa. RainDear holds up a painting of a rainbow. Alicia has recorded a dissertation into Dragon-Maker, which Nigel asks her to turn off after the Dragon has finished reciting a beat poem: *crystalize-ize-ize the na-na-nadir/celestial-celestial power to the ze-ze-zenith/crystalize-ize-ize the ze-ze-zenith/ destroy-oy-oy the underbelly-belly-belly of the na-na-nadir.*

When Nigel gets to Vanessa, she picks up a small piece of fabric on which she has stitched the words *Find the Ritual* using the thread from her travel sewing kit. She expects Nigel will pass her by, but instead he riffs on it.

"This is profound. It's the recognition of the power of the primordial which is the well-spring of creativity. Sleep on the ritual, Vanessa, and it will come to you. Bring it to the front of your mind and you will see it."

"I already feel it," she surprises herself by speaking.

"What do you mean?"

"I already feel something tingling in my fingers. I just don't know what it is."

"Honour those fingers. They will lead you to it. Thank the power of the primordial for whatever it brings. It's the message you are meant to hear. Make a ceremony and you will discover the message."

—

The strings at the back of Vanessa's halter top tangle after she makes a ceremony of smoking the rest of the joint. The tingling in her forefinger and thumb is so strong she can barely handle the strings. Once she's got the top on properly, she digs into her clothing drawer to find the leather shorts she made to go with it. She pulls them on and feels so full of excitement and energy, she stamps out a dance in her room. The fringes on the halter jiggle throughout her body as she runs outside.

She has to slow down, this is too stimulating. She has not felt this charged in years. She decides she better head to the refuge of the Laurel Bush garden. As she pushes open the gate, she pulls out a seed head that's stuck in the slats. It looks like a small human face with exploding hair. She is sitting under the apple tree pondering it, when one of the gardeners walks in her direction.

"What is this?" she extends the head toward him.

"It's from an ornamental onion called *Allium Schubertii*. It's named after the composer."

"It looks like him."

"I guess. I don't know what Schubert looks like," he says.

"Like this."

"Really?" He laughs and moves toward a pile of tubers that resemble tiny twisted human bodies. He begins to sort, discarding various fleshy ones that seem perfectly fine to Vanessa. She does not like to watch the cast-offs pile up like corpses.

"What are these?" she asks.

"Dahlia tubers."

"Why are you throwing some away?"

"We have lots, and some of these have a little mold on them."

She picks one of the freshest and biggest looking tubers from the reject pile and fits the stem of the Schubertii head into its neck.

"Look. He lives," she says. "Schubert rocks."

The gardener smiles.

Pleased with her creation, Vanessa stays to breathe in the life-affirming smell of the compost heaped behind the gardener. She looks over the gardenscape and wonders how she'd missed so much of it until now. The majestic blue delphinium at the end of the row looking out to sea. Lush bushes of cosmos, paper-white and bubblegum-pink, wavering in the wind. She strolls the rows of kale, carrots, chard, and beets. With her mind full of colour and life, she walks back toward the A-frame.

She places Schubertii on the pillow of her bed and goes outside to stand on her stoop to listen for the triangle. Its ring signals the start of a stream of couples—coupledom in costume—all headed for the dining hall for one last dinner before a rave in the woods. In the first minute a man dressed as a Buddhist monk, his wife as a geisha, a couple in snorkel gear possibly portraying divers from 'The Life Aquatic with Steve Zissou', and the bird-headdress pair, walk by. Vanessa feels hollowed out with a desire to participate in their ritual. At the bottom of her hollowness, she starts walking toward the nude artist's cottage.

Until she breaks through the canopy of foliage around his cabin she believes she's mostly on this trek to buy more wine. But as soon as she sees him sitting naked at his easel, she knows it's his company she's seeking.

"Well look who it is," he says. "My friend the scaredy cat."

Vanessa comes around the deck to have a look at his painting. She recognizes the scene. "That's the beach in front of Laurel Bush, isn't it?"

"Yes, the sward."

"A sward? What's that?"

"It means a grassy place. I like this spot because it's at the ocean where there are remnants of an orchard. Kind of a metaphor for civilization meeting the wild."

"It's good," she says.

"Yep. This one is turning out okay. I think they'll take it at the gift shop. Have a seat." He gestures toward the empty cedar chair.

She doesn't protest. She watches while he makes a few more strokes, then cleans his brush.

"Excuse me," he says rising from his chair.

"Sure. I didn't mean to intrude."

"You're not."

When he returns, he's wearing pants and a green t-shirt with yellow lettering that says *Take It All Off*.

"You didn't have to dress for me," she says.

"I know, but it's good to be formal when I have a visitor. Or did you want to buy some more wine?"

"I thought I did. But now that I'm here I'm okay just visiting, if you are. What's your name by the way?"

"Finn."

"I'm Vanessa."

When Finn offers her tube steaks and potato chips for dinner, she agrees. Hot dogs roasted over the fire on sticks that Finn has sharpened with his penknife taste surprisingly delicious, especially after a week of all-organic. As the sun sets, the two of them are comfortable burning coloured marshmallows on the ends of the sticks (all but the pink ones, which Finn has piled in a discard heap declaring "they're spiked with red dye no. 4"). He blows out a green marshmallow that he's caught on fire, and pops it into his mouth.

"Oh boy," he says. "Too hot." He munches and tries to get cool air into his mouth at the same time. It looks funny and they laugh. When he finishes with the marshmallow, he comes and stands behind Vanessa putting his hand very lightly on her bare back at the spot that would touch her heart if he were to drill through to the front of her chest. It makes her shoulders open like a dove's wings. For a second she thinks she'll pass out if her wings touch anything.

"You must be cold," he says as his hand spreads across her back.

It surprises her when he leaves to disappear inside his cabin again. He returns with another *Take It All Off* t-shirt. "You can keep it," he says, "I have a few. A friend gave them to me from a recycling campaign he worked on for the island."

"Thank you. A souvenir," she says.

She puts the shirt on and Finn says, "What's bugging you, honey?"

Vanessa doesn't know how to answer. Despite his youthful vigour, he is likely as old as she is, so she can't be rude and say, 'I don't like being the age I am.' But then, she says it anyway.

"Ha. I'm sure I have you bested by a couple of years," he says. "It's not so bad."

"Okay, then I don't like being the age I am and alone. And coming on this retreat has made me believe I am not a nice person. I can't *celebrate* like the others."

"Celebrate. Hogwash. Sometimes it's not the right time to celebrate. Not everything has to be pumped over the top."

"I know. But somewhere along the way I lost the ability to look inward and find any of the good stuff."

"It's in there. Don't be so hard on yourself and you won't be hard on others."

Vanessa takes a pink marshmallow from the discard pile and shoves it onto the end of her stick to hold to the flame.

Finn laughs. "You don't have to commit suicide over this."

They sit together in silence for a time. Then she stands, and he does, too. They hug. She breathes him in. She breathes him out, and that's all that's required. Nothing pumped over the top. Nothing to celebrate. It just is. They feel nice together but that's it.

"Well I should go," she finally says.

"Wait. I want to give you a real souvenir of your visit."

He disappears inside and comes out with a burlap bag. "It's a ritual I go through to see what people pull out. Tells me about their spirit side."

"Really? We're supposed to be working on ritual at the workshop."

"Well go ahead. Plunge in and find out who you are."

"Ow," Vanessa exclaims when something spears the end of her finger. It hits at the spot that hasn't stopped tingling since morning. She pulls out what looks like a porcupine quill with a duck feather stuck to it.

"Huh. Two for one," Finn says.

"I think I'm meant to take the quill," she smiles.

"Okay. I found that on Vancouver Island in Strathcona Park. Porcupines are rare around here. It suits you though. A bit prickly on the outside, but rare and radiant on the inside. Yes?"

"Yes. And always prepared." Vanessa waives her flashlight along the path in front of her as a gesture of farewell.

"Okay. Shine on, beauty," Finn says. "It's been a slice."

The triangle wakes Vanessa a half hour earlier than usual. The last morning wakeup is designed to give everyone time to clear the rooms before breakfast. She's in no hurry to rise. She can still feel the pressure of Finn's hand on her back. She enjoyed the hardness of his middle finger pressing near her spine.

When she finally does get up, she uses her time to gather everything together from the A-frame and get it out to the car. She plops Schubertii with his wild onion hair and dahlia body onto the passenger seat. Company for the trek back to the airport.

After a final breakfast of organic eggs and cornbread, she heads to Cedar Hall for the wrap-up. Nigel, who is apparently out of steam altogether, has little to say. For his parting shot, he invites people to tell one another what they are grateful for and besides the usual *grateful for the group*, *grateful for the wisdom of the leader*, there is one odd comment from Alicia who sidles up to Vanessa for a private word.

"I'm grateful for your coldness," Alicia whispers. "It helped stop what could have been a very emotional experience for me."

As Vanessa backs out of the parking lot, she uses only thoughts that serve her well. Surely I heard wrong. What Alicia meant to say was 'grateful for your coolness.' Big difference in such a small temperature change—cold to cool. She decides to stick with her reinterpretation and forget about it.

She follows the green fingerboards to the ferry. The trip seems a lot faster on the way out than it had on the way in.

Once she's safely on the ferry, no scratches on her rental, she has a clear view of the Strait. Next to her is Donna and Sarah's blue minivan. Donna helps Sarah out of the van so she can get a better look at the scenery. Sarah moves awkwardly without the wheelchair and Megabyte is anxious in the back seat. They move toward the ferry's rail. Donna has done something different with her hair, hers no longer matches Sarah's. Hers is curled and adorned with small jewels and seashells that catch the sunlight, where Sarah's hangs straight behind the usual hairband. Both look good. As the shoreline advances, there is an unmistakable love passing between them. Vanessa feels a twinge of compassion, and some regret. These women have a real relationship and she had not been fair and openhearted with any of the people on the couple's retreat. She remembers how it feels to have a real relationship. She had one for many years with Tom, and the good parts of that will never get taken away. It's a strength she carries with her.

But then there is Schubertii. She knows now he is not Schubert, he is some other musician, a bass player who travels with his scent and a quiver of instruments. She extracts the porcupine quill from her wallet. Her hand shakes. She waits for it to settle with the quill frozen in midair over the carcass, one end fitting neatly into the tingling spots on her forefinger and thumb. She moves her hand back and sinks the quill into the flesh of the tuber. She is elated to have committed.

— Part Two —

BEFORE THEN

ACORN

Her instructions were precise but unclear. Mrs. Bridgeman the grade eight teacher said, "The project is due no later than first bell on the Tuesday after Thanksgiving weekend. Thanksgiving is in October in Canada. Grades will be based on originality and an understanding of botanical science."

Her bouffant moved like a chiffon cloud in front of the blackboard as she wrote the due date—October 10, 1972. When she finished, she clapped her hands free of chalk dust. Mrs. Bridgeman hated anything messy.

Everyone knew when Thanksgiving was, but Mrs. Bridgeman, a transplanted American, rarely missed an opportunity to point out the differences between her country and Canada. There was no first and second bell in the school either. First bell was it, but she always mentioned it as if none of her students were strong on the basics.

The due date itself was clear. It was the botanical science part that scared Vanessa. It made her think of her dead grandmother and how *science couldn't save her.* She'd heard her father say so as he'd stood by his mother's casket at the funeral home that July. Vanessa's Aunt Marion, her father's younger sister, quietly sobbed when he'd said it. Vanessa watched all of this from behind. Her mother wouldn't let her near the casket. "It's too traumatizing," she'd said. But it was worse for her peering between the adults when all she could see was her Granma's nose and bosom.

Afterward at home, her mother said to her father, "Your sister Marion is full of guilt for the abuse she rained down on your mother. She doesn't know whether to be sad or delighted she's gone." Vanessa knew she wasn't supposed to have heard this, but it was hard not to hear everything that got said in their cramped two-bedroom apartment. Her father answered quietly. "Leave Marion out of this."

The conversation confused Vanessa. How could abuse rain? What was the science behind that? And might it have saved her Granma if abuse had not rained? The more she learned about science, the more it seemed beyond her. She'd only gotten a C minus on her first science test, and she'd studied hard for it. Mrs. Bridgeman wrote on her paper: *Fundamental misunderstanding of the sticky pistil.*

She'd misspelled the word as pistol, but other than that she thought she'd gotten it right. When she asked at the dinner table how the pistil in a flower works, her father said, "That's when the plant gets a boner." He was a little drunk, and her mother picked up the plates smeared with macaroni and ketchup, and started banging them into the kitchen sink. "Come and dry, Vanessa," she barked.

Vanessa knew a boner had to do with boys from listening to them talk at recess. Up until dinner she'd been pretty sure the pistil was a female part of the flower, but maybe that was her fundamental misunderstanding. Maybe she had things mixed up about sex.

On the way home from school on the Friday, Charlotte, who lived in one of the houses across the street from Vanessa's apartment building, talked about what she was going to do on the weekend. "Mom is taking me to Cloverdale Mall to look at clothes and makeup. She promised I could get a new pair of Levi's. Then we'll probably go to the Pine Room for supper. Dad has an account there." Charlotte's parents were divorced, but her father still paid for everything. Vanessa was jealous of the relationship Charlotte had with her mother—she'd never been shopping for makeup with her own mother—though, she did try to imagine what could have been so terribly wrong with Charlotte and her mother for the father to leave them.

The two girls didn't walk home together often. Charlotte was way cooler than Vanessa, but she risked rejection and ran to catch up with her because there were only two weekends to go before the science project was due.

"What do you think you'll do for science?" Vanessa asked.

"I'm going to make a Bristol board display with some pretty leaves. My Nana showed me how to press them."

"How do you press leaves?"

"You put them between waxed paper. If you were going to buy new Levi's would you get bellbottoms or overalls?"

"I don't know. Are you allowed to wear pants with a fly?"

"Course. I can wear whatever I want."

"Nice."

On the Saturday morning, Vanessa found a roll of waxed paper beside the utensils in the kitchen drawer. She didn't want to copy Charlotte, but she was curious what pressed leaves looked like. She folded over a towel from the bathroom two times, and put it on the counter. Down on her hands and knees she fetched the iron from beside the waffle maker they never used, and plugged it in. She waited for the iron to heat up and decided if this worked, she could write descriptions of each tree on a leaf-shaped piece of paper and stick it beside the matching pressed leaf. She'd been first to receive the ironing merit badge in her Brownie pack, so she knew not to set the iron too high until she'd experimented with her material. What she didn't know was that even at the lightest setting, waxed paper would melt.

When the square made a singeing sound and a shriveling piece of waxed paper with a curling maple leaf would not shake loose from the iron, she unplugged it and ran to her mother in the bedroom. She held up the mess. "I'm sorry, the iron burnt the paper."

Her mother looked up from the pot of nail varnish she was using to apply flaming fuschia to her fingernails and said, "Oh my god. You've ruined the iron. Put it there." She pointed to her bureau but there was no empty spot, so Vanessa pushed the stacked laundry to make a space. A pile of bras and underwear toppled and fell to the ground. "Don't touch my things, Vanessa," her mother wailed. "No more from you now. Go. Shut the door. And the iron did not burn the paper. You did."

Vanessa wanted to ask for help with the project, but knew she had to wait for another day. She wished her Granma was around to explain how to press leaves.

The next week over lunch in the gym some of the kids were discussing the science project. Vanessa hadn't been asked to join in, but she listened from the end of the table while she sipped on her milk carton and ate the Cheez Whiz and olive sandwich she'd made herself that morning. Carl explained his experiment using dyed water to show how a plant's capillaries pull the water up the stem into the flower head. "My mom bought some carnations for me to try. They worked great, but I think I'll get her to buy daisies for the project. I can make daisies any colour I want."

She liked the idea of dyeing flowers but had no idea what kind of dye to use. She knew her mother had started to colour the greying roots of her brown hair with a product called Miss Clairol. She was trying to go blonder to make her Mia Farrow pixie cut look better after her father had said the cut didn't work for her. "Maybe before you gained weight but not now," he said. "Your face is too round."

Vanessa found the Miss Clairol in the bathroom cupboard beside the new storage place for the iron. Except for a tiny bit of burnt paper still stuck to the edge, the iron looked fine. She picked the paper off the iron and opened the box of dye. The squeeze bottle inside contained an inky solution, darker than she expected for the blonde result. The smell was piercing. She wrinkled her nose and poured a little of it into one of the plastic drinking glasses and added some water. She ran down the building's two flights of stairs and out the front door to pick the last of the marigolds struggling since summer in the front garden.

She stuck five of the best marigolds in the solution. Because she didn't want anyone to see she'd taken dye from her mother's box, she shoved the glass under her bed and didn't peek again until after supper. When she did look, the marigolds were burnt like marshmallows. But the experiment was working.

The next night her father came home from work in a jovial mood that changed after her mother snapped at him. "You've been out drinking on a work night," she said. Still he tried to be lighthearted and pulled a neon-green plastic disc called a Frisbee from his briefcase. "Let's play," he said. "Look at this. We finally got the distribution rights." He glided the disc with some speed across the living room. It hit the doorframe at Vanessa's bedroom, angled off it and skidded under her bed. "Damn," he said, "I'm getting good at this."

A sludgy liquid seeped out from under the bed and along the cracks of the parquet floor into the living room.

"What is that?" her mother shrieked.

"Oh, no. It's my science experiment." Vanessa ran to her room and scooped the sodden marigolds from under the bed. Dye covered her hand and the side of her arm. When she wiped her face to get hair out of her eyes, the murky solution smeared across her mouth and nose.

"Jesus Christ, Vanessa," her mother said, "is that my hair dye you used?"

"Yes."

"What a waste. Now I'm going to be a fatty forever."

"Huh? What does hair dye have to do with getting fat, Mom?"

"I'm trying to look good, and you're setting everything back. Besides, it's your fault I'm fat, you know."

Vanessa felt stung and confused. Her father looked at her and said, "It's okay, sweetheart," then he wheeled around and said to her mother, "C'mon. You know you lost your baby fat a long time ago. Vanessa's twelve already."

Unrelated to anything, her mother sighed and said, "I need a job. But what job?"

Next day during health class, Mrs. Bridgeman told everyone to put their hands on the desk for inspection. When she got to Vanessa, she said, "Your nails are filthy. And when was the last time you washed your face properly?" Vanessa didn't know how to explain the filth was hair dye, that she had tried her best to wash it off. By the time she finally spoke to say, "I'll do better next time," Mrs. Bridgeman had moved down the aisle.

That afternoon after lunch, there was a titter of excitement when Mrs. Bridgeman wheeled the big projector into the classroom. The film on the reel was huge. Everyone loved it when they watched a movie during socials. It was so much better than studying the atlas or looking at food charts for India or Uganda and other places no one had ever been to.

The film started with the silent flash of a nuclear bomb. Vanessa sat stunned looking at the black and white image and listening to the projector click. Usually the sound was soothing. Today it was more like an angry typist hammering at a keyboard. The images went from bad to revolting. Dead dogs in the street, old people crying, blind children their faces melted. The movie seemed to take forever. Vanessa was greatly relieved when a flapping announced the end of the reel.

After Mrs. Bridgeman turned the flailing machine off, she tried to have a class discussion about the bomb. She spelled Hiroshima on the blackboard, but everyone was quiet. She clapped her hands free of chalk dust extra loud. Finally Bettina spoke up. "It was very sad. Everything was burned. The pets, the trees, the dragonflies and the buildings." Mrs. Bridgeman thanked her, and wheeled the projection cart out of the room. While she was gone, no one talked. Not even Stephen got out of his seat to run around and bug people. Vanessa hated it when Stephen came up close. His breath smelled of something rotten, like an old person, but not quite. It was his second time in grade eight.

She lay in bed that night and thought about the liquefied eyes of the children in Hiroshima. She had nightmares about mushroom clouds, blast waves, bald children vomiting, and charred dragonflies. It was the first time she remembered a dream having a soundtrack—blasts and thundering growls that turned into snarling dogs. Nuclear fission was a part of science she definitely did not want to understand.

The second morning after more bad dreams, she told her mother she couldn't go to school because she felt like throwing up. Her mother looked unconcerned and said if she didn't feel better by lunch she could come home. She walked to school and wondered if there was a connection between the dreams and all her failing science projects.

On the Friday of Thanksgiving weekend, her father came home and told Vanessa and her mother he'd been fired. "The buggers waited until 4 o'clock to tell me. After I'd already filled the car for next week's sales trip. They gave me a week's salary and no expenses." He threw the keys to the station wagon down on the kitchen counter and took a beer from the fridge. The bottle made a sharp pop when he snapped it open.

Vanessa woke early the next morning. Her parents were still asleep and she didn't want to sit alone in the apartment with the smell of stale pizza and cigarettes in beer bottles, so she went outside, past the shopping plaza and across the road down to the Humber ravine. She got down on her haunches at the riverbank and poked around looking for crayfish near the shore. When she found one, it made her think of Kenny, the boy who used to live in the apartment next door. Kenny had taught her how to handle the creatures. "Be gentle," he said, "hold them in the centre so the pincers don't get you."

She picked the crayfish up by its middle. It waved its tiny arms and bent its head back to try to pinch her. She could feel its innards and loosened her grip. Its searching eye on the end of the tiny stalk moved in a quiet pivot looking for the source of its confounding situation. She knew how bad it felt to be in need of something and yet not quite able to see what it was you needed. She set the crayfish on the sand. She missed Kenny. He was a grade ahead of her and he knew everything. He'd know what she could do for the project. But his mother had moved him away with her to Vancouver.

She watched the crayfish's arching body and for a second thought she could bring it to class for the project and to demonstrate how to handle one properly. Then she remembered the chart Mrs. Bridgeman drew on the board in September. Biology was at the top, and the words botany and zoology were at the ends of the arms underneath. The crayfish was zoology, which they wouldn't be taking up until next term. She lifted the crayfish from the sand and placed it gently back into the river. It looked peaceful, and for a second she loved it.

She looked down the shoreline and spied a baby oak tree growing from an acorn lodged in the riverbank. Bingo. "Thank you, Kenny," she said out loud. "I'm going to find baby trees and take them to school."

When she got back to the apartment she could hear her father clearing his throat in the bathroom. He sounded like the old Minster at the church trying to get his voice started. *Aa-aa-hem aa-aa-hem.* Then her father made a gross spitting sound. She saw her mother's back in the bed, turned away from the bedroom door. She wasn't moving. Vanessa tiptoed into the kitchen.

She quietly opened the utensil drawer searching for diggers. She pulled out the metal-edged soupspoon and the chicken carving knife. Not much, but the best she could come up with. Down the stairs, and out the side door of the building across the lane to the shopping center, where she scrounged in the garbage piled behind the florist's shop. She found six discarded pots. Five were cracked, but she could tape them together, and one was a shiny new black plastic that only needed a wash. From the rubbish in front of the smoke shop she dug out several used Popsicle sticks and shoved them in her pocket. She would write the names of the trees on the sticks, and hoped the green, red, orange and purple stains would scrub off.

Stephen from class loitered in front of the shop. He watched her dig through the garbage. "Why are you so weird?" he asked. Vanessa pretended not to hear him. He pulled out a cigarette and lit it, and she started to run toward the ravine with the pots, the spoon, and the carving knife in her hand.

She was still running when she got to where she'd seen the baby oak sprouting from the riverbank. She dug carefully around it, but some of the acorn fell away. She scooped extra mounds of dirt into the pot and jammed bits of the acorn on top. She decided this would be a really interesting thing to present to the class. How protection around life falls away so easily.

It took longer than she thought it would to find more baby trees, but eventually she'd uprooted a cedar, a pine of some sort—she'd have to identify which kind—a tiny tree she believed was a birch with one yellow leaf, and the prize, a sugar maple with three blazing leaves that she put into the shiny black pot. She couldn't find a sixth tree, but even so the five pots were too awkward for her to carry back in one go. She'd seen the lid of a cardboard box at the dumpster behind the florist. She pulled the pots into the brush by the river, so no one would steal them, and ran back to find the lid.

By the time she got everything back upstairs to the apartment her parents were watching the Stampeders and Tiger-Cats play football on TV. It was near the end of the fourth quarter. Beer bottles covered the coffee table in front of them, and the kitchen was a mess.

"What's that dirty stuff you've got with you?" her mother asked.

"My science project," she said.

"Not in here."

"Okay I'll put it under my bed."

"Not on your life. Not after the last mess you made."

"Then where?"

"Why are you such a difficult child?"

"Mom. Please, can you help me?"

Vanessa sat the box on the kitchen counter so she could wash the soupspoon and the carving knife and put them back in the drawer. She threw the Popsicle sticks in the water and gave them a good scrub. After she finished, she could see her father holding up the station wagon keys. "Here, kitten," he said, "put the stuff in the back of the car."

When her father first got the job with the toy company, he'd bought a used Country Squire station wagon with wood paneling and power windows. He needed the extra room for hauling samples on his sales trips, and it felt fancy to drive in the car with him and push a button to open the window. She opened the trunk and placed the trees behind the back seat. There was a box in the car with stuff from her father's office, a stapler, Scotch tape, and a bunch of papers, including a sheet of purple paper with a psychedelic flower sticker on it. When she pulled the paper from the box, she saw the words *All You Need Is Love* on the sticker and handwriting that said 'I used to wait for the weekends. Now I wait for Monday mornings'. The paper was signed, 'Rambling Rose'.

She wondered who Rose was, but put the paper back where she found it. She used the tape to seal the cracked flowerpots, and took a pen from her father's box to write the names of the trees on the sticks. She admired her bounty, then locked her treasures inside the car. She ran her hand along the car's luxurious wood paneling for good luck. Upstairs she gave her father the keys and went to her bedroom to read her science book and start working on the demonstration part of the project. That night in bed, she thought about how beautiful her trees looked when she closed the trunk. She was sure she would get an A, or maybe only an A minus because the popsicle sticks had not come as clean as she wanted. Still, A minus would be a good mark.

On Sunday when she looked through the car window, the trees seemed parched and she silently scolded herself for not watering them before locking them in. She asked for the keys, but no one answered. Her parents were in a stormy mood and she did not want to bother them so she searched for the keys by herself but couldn't find them. By the evening of Thanksgiving Monday, she was seriously concerned about the condition of the plants. When she peered through the back window of the station wagon, she could see the birch had dropped its leaf, and the slender oak was leaning precariously. She asked her father again for the keys. He put his hands into his pocket and pulled out nothing.

"Don't know," he said.

"Please, can you look for them? I really need to water my trees."

"Sometimes you make no sense," her mother said. She was drinking crème de menthe and eating potato chips with dill dip and cookies for her Thanksgiving dinner.

"Please! Just tell me where to look then." Vanessa pleaded. She could feel hives moving up her arms. This had not happened to her in a long time.

"Here, put a little of this on some ice cream and relax," her father said. He held out the crème de menthe bottle. In the kitchen Vanessa gave the bottle's contents a sniff and didn't like the oversweet minty smell, so she only ate ice cream for dinner. When she put the dirty bowl in the sink, her mother commanded, "Wash the bowl properly and bring the bottle back."

Vanessa was confused. Usually her mother was nagging her father not to drink. This time, her mother seemed drunker than he did. As she carried the bottle toward her parents, she tried to wipe off the sticky sides with her fingers but the bottle slipped and fell on the floor. A pool of green syrup poured onto the rug.

"Shit, Vanessa," her mother said. "You were dropped on me like a bomb, you know. I never wanted kids and now I know why."

It was the weirdest Thanksgiving ever.

At night, she lay in bed and worried the trees were dying. She got out of bed and went to the window to look down on them in the parking lot. The streetlight shone into the back of the station wagon like a guardian angel. "Mercy," she said and blew a kiss toward the trees. Her Aunt Marion used the word a lot and she hoped it would smooth things out, make bad things more okay. Later, she woke to her parents quarrelling. Her mother sounded altered. She heard her say, "So that's it then?" and a door slam.

Vanessa had trouble falling asleep again wondering what *it* was. To take her mind off *it*, she thought about what to wear for the presentation the next day. She decided on her best pink skirt with the matching cardigan sweater. Aunt Marion had bought the set for her. Since Marion was an artist and knew colours well, Vanessa was pretty sure she would look her best in the outfit. Aunt Marion was lots of fun and Vanessa entertained herself waiting for sleep by thinking about going to the mall with her, looking at makeup, maybe getting a new hairstyle. Her last thought before sleep was that she should have asked Aunt Marion to help with the project. She would have made it look spectacular. What was wrong with her? Why had she not thought to ask?

She woke early. Her parent's bedroom door was closed and she did not want to make them mad by waking them to ask for the keys. She tried not to think about why someone had slammed the door in the middle of the night.

She searched everywhere and finally looked in the bag of frozen peas where she knew her mother sometimes hid the keys from her father when she thought he was too drunk to drive. She was relieved to find them, and skipped down the stairs to the car where her mood dissolved. The oak tree's leaves, which were already brown, looked crinkled and dead. The pine had dropped some of its needles. The birch leaf was shriveled on top of the soil around the tiny trunk. Only the maple was healthy and beautiful, and the cedar was still sweet. When she got the car door open, she rubbed the top of the cedar gently. She enjoyed the feeling under her fingers, almost as if the baby tree was saying good morning to her. She pulled the box out of the car.

The box got heavier and heavier as she went. Close to the school playground, she dropped it. The cedar fell ahead of the others, and the tip snapped when the box hit it. Some of the oak's acorn shell scattered on the road beside the birch leaf, which blew away. Pieces of gravel stuck to the decomposing mess of acorn, and more of it turned to mush when she picked the tiny stones off.

At the school drinking fountain she tried to revive the trees, but water seeped out of the corners of the box and made a dirty stain on her best pink skirt. She sat in her seat in class with her hands folded over the mess and hives crawled up her arms, again.

When it came time for the demonstration, Bettina asked to go first. She held up a series of drawings of leaves and read a poem that used the words *brief, sheaf* and *relief* to rhyme with *leaf.* She told the class she drew the leaves using her Laurentian pencil crayon set with 117 different colours.

Mrs. Bridgeman said, "Beautiful drawings, Bettina."

Carl went next. He explained how the capillaries worked to pull the dye into the heads of the daisies turning the flowers into all the colours of the rainbow. "Plants and humans are similar," he said. "Liquid is carried in both by capillaries, but in humans the heart does the pumping where the miracle of plants is that they do it themselves. Transpiration is caused by evaporation from the plant's mesophyll cells." When he was finished, he presented the rainbow bouquet to Mrs. Bridgeman, who cooed and made a *Mmmmm-wah* sound in his direction as he sat down. Vanessa wondered whether it was better to have a heart or mesophyll cells. Her Granma died because of her heart.

Rudy Elias put up his hand and asked if he could present next.

Everybody used Rudy's first and last names when they referred to him, even though he was the only Rudy in the school. He was from Egypt and his real name was Ruwaid. He was pudgy, but had beautiful, smooth looking skin. Vanessa didn't really know him except that he lived in the biggest house, up on the hill, and he got picked up after school in a car, with a fancy ornament of a leaping tiger, that a man who wasn't his father drove. "It's a chauffeur," Bettina had told her one day.

Rudy wasn't popular, but Vanessa felt a kinship toward him. Maybe because both of them got ignored a lot. But there was something more. When she watched him bent over his book writing intently, his cursive elegant, she felt calm. She often found herself glancing at the side of his face when she knew he wasn't looking. For some reason his cheekbone took her to the edge of the ravine where the most fun adventures always began. Secretly she liked him quite a bit, but she couldn't risk showing him friendship when the rules of engagement around social bounds were so tight at the school.

She looked up and smiled at Rudy when he stood to walk toward the front. He smiled back. He looked tense. He was carrying a box covered in an exotic silky cloth. He took the cloth off with a flourish and stood nervously grinning. Inside sat six matching shiny black pots. Same as the shiny one Vanessa had found behind the florist's at the shopping center. Each of his pots held a beautiful plant. He said they were called Norway pine, box plant, eelgrass, magnolia, chrysanthemum and hibiscus. The class giggled when he said, "For many years women were not allowed to drink hibiscus tea in Egypt because Egyptians believed it made them too interested in sex."

Stephen yelled, "Right on," after Rudy added, "My mother drinks hibiscus tea all the time for her blood pressure." He finished his presentation by giving everyone in the class a chrysanthemum that he brought out from another box he'd kept hidden under his desk. "The mum brings power and grace," he said as he gave Mrs. Bridgeman hers. She blushed.

When it was Vanessa's turn she brought her box of tiny trees to the front and started by apologizing that her box got wet. She had meant to go on and explain what each of the trees were called and how she had dug them up, but she was rattled by the mess on her skirt, and by Rudy's beautiful presentation. She managed only to say, "I have examples of birch, maple, cedar, oak and pine—and this is not just any old pine, it's a white pine. I looked it up." She ended quickly saying, "The most interesting thing is the oak tree grows from an acorn. I'm sorry when I dropped the box the acorn turned to mush."

Mrs. Bridgeman said, "Vanessa, you should never start or end a presentation with an apology. It turns the audience off." She was grateful Mrs. Bridgeman at least had not said anything about the mess on her skirt.

The next day, when everyone got to class, Mrs. Bridgeman had arranged all the presentations around the perimeter of the classroom in order of grades. Carl's bouquet was first, followed by Rudy's beautiful box. Charlotte's was near the top because she had set up her Bristol board of pressed leaves like the old-fashioned botanical chart Mrs. Bridgeman had brought from the American Museum of Natural History. Even Bettina's project, which had nothing to do with science, was in the middle of the group.

Vanessa scanned the room and saw that hers was dead last, next to Stephen's, which was second to last. Stephen had written two sentences on a sheet of paper and traced his hand below with a drawing of some sort of leaf inside it. The worst of it was that the beautiful maple tree from her box had been moved into Rudy's box. She thought she was going to pass out when she saw this. She had plans for that tree when she got home. She was going to give it to her father who was feeling so sad about losing his job.

All afternoon she picked at the hives on her arm and when she went to the back at the end of the day to grab her box, Mrs. Bridgeman came behind her. "I think you could have done better, Vanessa. Dead sticks in dirty containers do not show respect for science." Then Mrs. Bridgeman, who was always looking for what she called the "teachable moment" added, "And used Popsicle sticks are not sanitary. We'll be taking up sanitation in health class next week. You will learn how kids can pass worms to each other when they share food."

Out of nowhere, Vanessa exploded. "I washed the Popsicle sticks. AND the trees are not dead. I dug them up myself. They're alive. I tried. It's not easy, you know." In her fury she uprooted the oak by its stem. It came out of its pot with several pieces of acorn still attached. When Vanessa saw the tree really was alive, out of respect for science, she carefully dug it back in, scooping dirt with her fingers and deliberately not looking at Mrs. Bridgeman.

"Oh, you should have explained that," Mrs. Bridgeman said. She switched the order of Vanessa's project with Stephen's. "Wash your hands in the girl's bathroom on your way out," she said.

"Leave Stephen's where it is," Vanessa said. She switched the projects back before picking up her box. It felt good for once that Stephen was not last.

She stalked down the hall, past the girl's bathroom, and out of the school. She walked along the lineup of waiting cars and was surprised to see her Aunt Marion's in front of the Rudy Elias car. Her aunt poked her head out the window and yelled, "*You-who,* over here, sweetie."

When Vanessa opened the car's door, Aunt Marion said, "Oh what interesting things you have. Maybe we can plant those at the house. In the garden. Since you don't have a yard, that is. You know I've always thought your parents could have done better about getting a nice house with a patch of grass. But I guess it isn't going to happen now. Mercy. We'll see where everyone ends up after this. Lucky your mother can go to her brother's to live for a while. You're going to spend the week at my house, sweetie. Won't that be fun. Until things settle down. Who knew it was that bad? Put those in the backseat, will you, sweetie."

Whenever Aunt Marion used the word sweetie a lot, it meant she was trying hard to make bad things good. At least she recognized the *dead sticks* Vanessa had with her were actually alive. Her aunt's blonde hair was long and straight, and she'd recently added Carnaby Street bangs to modernize her look. She was wearing a peasant blouse and bell-bottom blue jeans. With the new hairstyle, she looked like the model Jean Shrimpton and Vanessa was proud to be related to her. But she didn't like the sound of whatever it was Aunt Marion was going on about. It sounded like she was going to live for a while with Marion who'd moved into her Granma's house. And it made her stomach tight when she opened the back door of the car to see a pile of her things from the apartment heaped on the seat. Her fuzzy turquoise bathrobe was wrapped around her socks, her underwear and most of her skirts and tops. As she slammed the back door, the neon green Frisbee fell from the top of the stack and disappeared under the front seat.

"What's so bad?" Vanessa asked after she climbed into the front seat.

"Oh you know, grownup stuff," Aunt Marion said. "Mercy my mother isn't here to see this."

"See what?"

"The breakdown. It must have been terrible for you."

Suddenly, there was a knock at the window. It made both Aunt Marion and Vanessa jump in their seats. Rudy Elias was standing beside the car holding out Vanessa's maple tree. He yelled through the window. "I think this is yours. Our gardener didn't buy this one."

Vanessa opened the car door to take the plant from him. She put it at her feet instead of getting out to open the back door. She was embarrassed for him to see her clothes piled on the seat.

"Is this your mother?" Rudy asked.

"No, it's my aunt. Aunt Marion, this is Rudy."

"Nice to meet you, young man," Aunt Marion said.

"You too," he said.

After Rudy left, Aunt Marion asked, "You know someone with a Jag?" She didn't wait for Vanessa to answer before she put her car in reverse and backed up to stop beside Rudy's car. She motioned to Vanessa to roll down her window. The driver in Rudy's car powered his window down. Her aunt called over to him, "Thanks for returning the plant. Name's Marion."

The driver in the other car nodded his head and said, "Lateef."

"Maybe see you again, Lateef," Aunt Marion said. Lateef and Rudy both smiled. Vanessa did, too.

Aunt Marion put her car in gear and drove forward. She turned to Vanessa. "See that's how you do it. That's how you meet a man. Takes nerve, but worth it."

Vanessa never did answer her Aunt's question. She didn't know what a jag was other than when her mother complained she was not to go on another "crying jag". She seemed to have a fundamental misunderstanding of what was going on and for a moment thought her heart might stop. All she knew to do was to wait for someone to tell her what she was supposed to feel.

Slow Song, Fast Car

'SAM CROW FINALLY GRADUATED - 1982' was painted in midnight blue letters on the cement abutment up Highway 12 near where Old Coldwater Road crossed the Orillia town line. Whoever painted it had committed an offence under the public property laws, but the Ontario Department of Highways didn't get around to sandblasting the testament off until two years after it first appeared. Everybody knew Sam was not the offender.

Vanessa McMorrin was the student teacher assigned to the Grade 13 English class the last time around for Sam. The Tuesday after Easter weekend was her first day in the classroom, and she was to be teaching off and on until the end of the school year. Her sponsor teacher, Mr. Kershaw, asked her to come to the back of the room right before her first class was to begin.

"I will be overseeing from here. I will call you Miss McMorrin, not Vanessa, as will all the students," he said. She listened while he told her he'd had trouble the year before with a student teacher named Liam who became too familiar with the students. "In my view, it started when he let the students address him by his first name. Unsuitable behaviour."

As the students began to file in, Vanessa noticed one who looked a bit older. Sam sat on the left side of class, three rows from the front, quiet dark eyes. At twenty-two, she was only a couple of years older than he was.

Stiff with nerves for her first class, she wrote her name in white chalk on the board then read from William Butler Yeats' 'The Second Coming'.

Turning and turning in the widening gyre
The falcon cannot hear the falconer;

Things fall apart; the centre cannot hold;
Mere anarchy is loosed upon the world,
The blood-dimmed tide is loosed, and everywhere
The ceremony of innocence is drowned;
The best lack all conviction, while the worst
Are full of passionate intensity.

She asked, "Any ideas what Yeats meant by these lines?"

The question fell on fallow ears, too many terms of Mark Twain or whatever was easiest from the high school curriculum. She walked back and forth in front of the chalkboard. She should think of a peppier, more hip way of asking the questions, somehow appeal to the students. As she thought this, she simultaneously shied away from being too hip, worried she'd be tarred with the same unsuitable brush as Liam.

"Think about it," she urged. "Think about things falling apart. Imagine a blood-dimmed tide. What could it mean?"

Her voice trembled. She steadied herself by holding one finger on the top of the desk. Finally a girl in the front row raised her hand and stood. She wore a clingy purple, Paisley mini-skirt that showed too much thigh. Her knees were pasty and helpless looking.

"I think he means things fall apart when the best people don't care." The girl slumped back into her seat, as if exhausted by the effort.

"Good answer, uh... Patsy."

She had to check the seating plan. "Sorry," she said, "I thought I'd memorized everybody's name. Anybody else have an idea? You don't need to stand in this class to speak."

This time Jamie Duke spoke up. "Hey. Why don't you skip this birdbrain stuff and get on to the cheese."

The bad boys in the class snickered. Vanessa didn't want to look directly at any of them. She knew Jamie was one of several feet-in-the-aisle-just-looking-for-a-lousy-pass types sitting at the back of the room. Mr. Kershaw had pointed them out before she'd gone to the front of the room. "Knuckle draggers," he'd said. "Ignore them. They'll try to get to you."

"What do you mean by cheese?" She directed her question to a spot on the wall behind Jamie.

"You know, like last year when we took up about that guy Willy. The one who made it with the broad who was always whining about silk stockings while raw music was playing."

Jamie pronounced the word raw as if it had about fifteen a's in it. It made the bad boys laugh, again. This time she surveyed the back row carefully and was arrested by the sight of a blonde girl seated next to Jamie. A beauty among a band of lynch men, she thought. Not supposed to be sitting there according to the seating plan.

When class ended, Jamie sauntered out the door, his arm heavy across the blonde's shoulders. He was handsome, in that baggy under the eye sort of way. He looked good with the blonde. When everyone was gone, Vanessa checked with Mr. Kershaw and found out the girl was Marnie Texada. "She's supposed to be on the right, up the side," he said. "But leave it the way it is."

She wanted to ask Mr. Kershaw if Liam had taught 'Death of a Salesman' to Jamie the year before, but didn't want it to look as if she was interested in any way other than educational. She was a little shocked at how grown up some of the boys in Orillia seemed. If she had to put a word to it, she would have said the boys looked experienced.

At lunchtime when Vanessa made her way to the staff room, Miss Daniels, the biology teacher, followed her through the door. Miss Daniels who was about fifty and dressed mostly in tweeds, hooted generally to everybody in the room, before she lowered herself into the seat next to Vanessa. She leaned in as if she had something highly confidential to disclose.

"I see you have Sam Crow in your class."

"Yes."

"He's mixed you know. His mother's a Chippewa. His father, a Scot I think. They didn't marry 'til Sam was nearly seven. Then the father took off a year later. That sort of makes Sam an illegitimate child, but a legitimate Indian. If you know what I mean."

"No, not exactly."

"Well Sam's mother lost her status when she married out-side, though Sam kept his. Her name got struck from the band register. She lost her free cigarettes, and everything. Even lost the right to live on the reserve. So Sam's kinda angry about that, I think. He said something to me about lost heritage once."

"It sounds like they sort of did lose something."

"Well, his mother doesn't see it that way. She told me at the supermarket, 'Only God has the power to determine who an Indian is, and only God can take that away.' She's tried to make Sam understand, but he lives somewhere in between. That's some kind of destiny, don't you think."

Vanessa wanted to ask what Miss Daniels meant by destiny, but she never seemed to stop talking even to take a breath. She went on and on about how the land on the reserve was largely useless and what a conundrum the whole status thing was. Then the bell rang, and she jumped up and was out the door before Vanessa had a chance to say anything other than "uh-huh" and "yuh".

Soon after 4 o'clock, Vanessa stepped out onto the street. It had been a tough day. She was exhausted and already questioning whether teaching was a good career choice for her. She blinked in the intensity of the late afternoon sunlight as she walked toward the bus stop in front of the school. Winter was hanging on, but unlike teaching she liked the feel of the town right from the start. It was a simple middle Ontario town, but it felt substantial somehow. The main street was lined with proud red brick buildings, and the high school built in the 60s, admittedly without a lot of soul, was open and bright.

As she turned to look for her bus, an older white Lincoln Continental screeched out of the school parking lot. The car came perilously close to where she was standing, the spare tire case sitting up on its rump like a ringworm. When the Continental sped past, she could see Jamie Duke behind the wheel and Marnie Texada snuggled next to him.

—

During lunch hours, Vanessa learned more than she ever imagined a teacher was supposed to know about her students. The ever-eager Miss Daniels filled her in, first about Jamie, how he lived the fast life, hung out with rough characters who drove stolen cars up from Buffalo filled with bales of marijuana. How he could drink whiskey fist to fist with the best of them. How he slept with Marnie on the weekends and knew where to get an abortion for anybody who wanted one.

Then about Marnie, how she lived with her mother and senile grandmother, 20 miles around the other side of the lake in tiny hamlet. How so far as anyone knew, there never had been a father in the household, and they made their money from running the Texada Roadside Café. According to Miss Daniels, the Café, Cooper's Bait & Gas, and two houses posed as the entire hamlet. The Café was at the bottom of a dip in the road where the lake seeped through the soil and made the air smell like dew worms in the summer.

"You should see Marnie's mother running that place," Miss Daniels said. "Breadstick thin legs wavering precariously over spiked heels while she flutters about filling coffee cups and balling up crumbs from the lunch counter in her hand. And that grandmother of Marnie's sitting behind the counter. Kind of freaky, watery blue eyes fronting a head of stone. Nothin' going on in there at all."

Vanessa had begun to admire Miss Daniel's way with words, so she did little to discourage the lunchtime talk. She heard that Marnie's mother, a pretend strict Catholic, had forbidden Marnie to date anybody except for Jamie. In her conspiratorial way, Miss Daniels told her, "Marnie's mother confided in me. You know, she said, 'That Marnie. She's got herself a meal-ticket there'. And I had to agree. Jamie's worth a fortune—an inheritance of over a million dollars! Though you sorta have to feel sorry for him, how he got it that is. No good both your parents up and dying before you've even graduated from high school."

"What happened?" Vanessa asked.

"Cancer, drugs, alcohol. You name it. They say the family made their money in the rubber business, but I don't know.

Seems to me there hasn't been enough rubber goods sold in this town to fill even one small bank account. So who knows where the money really comes from."

The stories dragged on, and so did winter through the month of April. The snow, the sky, and the lake, all the same leaden colour. But for a time, the English class achieved an easy sort of rhythm. A shuffling in and out of everyday life. Even Jamie seemed subdued by the monotony.

Vanessa didn't venture out much in the cold, except to go back and forth to school, and on the weekend to make the three block trek from her suite over the drugstore, with its dripping kitchen faucet and cracked ceiling, to the movie theatre. On Saturday the cinema brought in an art movie. She saw the movie 'Five Easy Pieces' three times, including the matinee. In the dark in the theatre during the third screening, she began to think the way to become as interesting as Jack Nicholson, or perhaps it was the way to capture the attention of someone as interesting as Jack, was to make rash decisions and fling herself into a long-distance journey with no determined end point.

After the movie alone in her suite, staring up at the crack that moved from the bathroom door across the living room ceiling to her bedroom door, she realized pulling herself out of the west end of Toronto and moving to Orillia had been exhausting, so maybe her journey should not include a succession of squalid bars and motels like Jack's. Yet she saw the gleam of burnished gold of some unknown destination on her horizon when she closed her eyes and let her mind wander. She was almost asleep and surprised herself when she drifted into intimate thoughts of Sam Crow. She did not want to become the next student teacher the staff talked about after she was gone, so she stuffed those feelings down and went to bed where the movie reel of her life clicked through her head. She jerked herself awake a few times, and twice she had to get up to drink water because of the three bags of salty popcorn she'd eaten at the movie. The second time she was up, the tap closed with a bang of the pipes and she took it as a warning shot. But for what?

The next week, the most excitement to be had was on the school basketball court. The boys' team had made it into the semi-finals of the Ontario championships. Their gym teacher and coach, a tall fit man named Tom Harringdon, had the kind of quiet determination that Vanessa thought might make the team take the championship. He was one of the few teachers who really seemed to have the kids' respect. Still they lost their semi-final match 101 to 99 to a team from Toronto, and Mr. Harringdon tried to rally school morale by promising a barbeque as soon as the weather cooperated. No one was much cheered by the prospect of charred hotdogs when the school fields still had crusts of snow on them. But everyone appreciated his effort.

When May and spring weather finally arrived, Vanessa was eager to get out and about. She decided to take the scenic bus trip that left from out front of the community centre on Saturday mornings. The tour went around the lake and stopped at the Texada Roadside Café for lunch. Even though at $7.95, the ticket was more than her budget afforded, she convinced herself it was well spent. She wanted to learn about the community where her students lived.

By the time the bus stopped at the Café, its door had been opened and closed so many times a fine layer of dust covered the table she sat at. She'd been traveling with a group of librarians from Barrie and a quiet couple from Huntsville. The couple barely spoke to one another, let alone to anyone else, so Vanessa took the seat at the end of their table. She'd placed an order for a toasted western sandwich when a motorcycle roared up in front of the Café. She turned toward the sound, and was surprised to see Sam on the back behind another man. Marnie's mother made a faint clucking sound when she looked out the window.

Vanessa rotated away from the window so Sam wouldn't see her. Once inside, Sam sat at the counter with his back to her, and she kept herself turned, so he wouldn't be embarrassed to meet his teacher in public. She heard Sam and his friend order steak sandwiches, homemade blueberry pie, and two cups of coffee. Marnie's mother treated them fine, until she came by for coffee refills and Sam asked, "Is Marnie around?"

Vanessa couldn't help but sneak a look. She watched Marnie's mother ball up a remnant of piecrust and drop it in front of Sam. Then she half filled the coffee cups, and hurriedly slapped the bill down.

She never did answer Sam's question. But Sam didn't need an answer. It was the weekend and everybody knew Marnie was with Jamie.

After Sam and his friend left the Café, Vanessa heard Marnie's mother say, "Shoot. I forgot to charge them for the pies. My fault. Makes me so nervous what might be going on there. Right mum?"

The words were wasted on the wind. Marnie's grandmother didn't even waiver.

The next week, Vanessa was reading to the English class from Steinbeck's 'The Red Pony'. She'd finished the passage about the pony colt staring from its stall at the young master whose throat was so swollen with love it was difficult for him to breathe. She set the book down and before she could pose a question, Sam put his hand up.

"I don't know much about reading, but I do know about the love of a horse that can pretty soon bring a swell to the neck. That guy Steinbeck's got that part right, okay."

Sam's way of speaking depended more on phrasing and colouring of sound than it did on vocabulary. Words sometimes seemed to come from high in the pines and other times from the depth of a marsh. This time, they came from the heart. He lowered his eyes when he finished speaking.

Jamie hollered from the back of the room. "That's some touching, man."

Sam ignored Jamie, but at the end of class he walked up to Jamie and said, "You ought'a think more about what things mean instead of the way they seem to be."

Jamie didn't acknowledge that he'd even heard Sam speak.

Two weeks later at the Spring Fair, Vanessa learned that Sam really did know about love for a horse. She sat in the stands of the riding ring directly behind Marnie and her best friend Sue Ellen. They were waiting for the horse show to begin when Sam came riding out wearing an intricately embroidered shirt with pearl snaps. He was astride an impressive chestnut stallion that looked nurtured and curried. Marnie and Sue Ellen made an excited giggle as he rode toward them. After Sam took a turn in front of them, Vanessa thought she caught a look in Marnie's eye that said she wanted to wander down one of the pasture roads and do it right there in the dust and the dirt with him.

"Isn't he delicious," she heard Marnie say to Sue Ellen.

"Don't be ridiculous. You got Jamie."

Marnie made an unintelligible sound in her throat and let the lids on her eyes drop. Like guillotines, Vanessa thought.

In the first week of June, when the wood violets were finished and the lilacs were in bloom, an electricity sparked the air. It positively crackled, the day Marnie came to class wearing new reading glasses. She asked to move up in the room and Vanessa said, "Take whatever empty seat is comfortable." Marnie chose the seat next to Sam. At the end of the lesson, Jamie walked up to Sam and pushed him against the doorjamb. He moved in close and hissed, "What was that all about, man?"

"I don't know what you're talking about," Sam said.

Jamie wheeled out the door without waiting for Marnie.

It was tense in class after that, and Vanessa found herself frequently referring to the final exam. She needed a sobering influence to keep a lid on things. Everybody was mightily relieved by the time the exam finally arrived and was written.

She never had any doubt Marnie would make it through, and she never really had a doubt about Jamie. But she did have a small fear when it came to Sam. Mr. Harris said he would do the grading seeing as it was the finishing line for the students.

She was no longer at the school as a student teacher the day she looked the marks up. She'd applied for and got the summer custodial job because she needed a decent summer salary. She'd decided teaching really was not her thing, and was going back to George Brown College to train in fashion design, a decision her mother did not support and one her father couldn't afford to assist her with. She was still able to roam the school as if nothing had changed, and got herself a cup of coffee from the staff room before going into the office to look at the results. The coffee tasted bitter burnt as she scanned the grade sheets looking for Sam's name. When she found it, a rush of relief. A glorious pass at 61. She was reviewing the rest of the grades, when the Vice-Principal, a small chirpy woman in a yellow pantsuit, came up behind her.

"Will you chaperone the graduation dance? Miss Daniels was supposed to do it, but she's going to Barrie for a wedding that weekend."

"When is it again?" Vanessa asked.

"Next Friday. At the Blue Heron Dance Hall. You know, down by Lake Couchiching."

"Sure."

The Vice-Principal didn't seem to know or care that Vanessa was no longer part of the teaching staff.

Nobody expected Sam to show. Jamie and Marnie were starting a slow dance to the searing Righteous Brothers' tune 'You've Lost that Loving Feeling' when he walked in. The Coca-Cola clock above the stage said it was almost midnight. Marnie didn't notice Sam until halfway through the song, and when she did she shifted her weight slightly and gave him a look like she was going to go over and do something nice for him. The song ended and Marnie disentangled from Jamie. She moved a couple of rhythmic steps toward Sam then stopped. Jamie said nothing, but everyone saw how for a second he lost his confident pose.

"What the hell you lookin' at, girl?" Jamie finally spoke.

"Nothing."

"The hell you're lookin' at nothin'. You're lookin' at that dumb chief."

"No, Jamie, I'm dancing with you."

"Who's your partner, Marnie? That's the thing. It's not who you dance with, it's who you want to give your goddam ass to that counts."

Suddenly Jamie was moving across the dance floor, his fists in a fury clenching and unclenching. He put his face up to Sam's, breathed in Sam's breath and spit it back out. Mr. Harringdon, the phys ed teacher, pushed his way between the two and hurled Jamie aside. Sam stood in the middle of the dance floor for a moment, then walked out. The screen door slapped behind him. Vanessa watched him pass by the side window, then followed. He looked so vulnerable outside by himself.

"Sam," she called.

"Yes." He turned toward her.

"Are you all right?"

"Good," Sam answered.

Then there was another voice in the mix. It was Mr. Harringdon holding the screen door open.

"Watch yourself," he said.

At first, Vanessa thought he was talking to Sam. She didn't move. He repeated himself. "Watch yourself, Vanessa." It shocked her to hear him use her first name. She didn't think he knew it. He nodded at her as she walked back inside. Something inside her shifted from five-easy-pieces-out-there-in-search-of-gold to safely-inside-but-bored-waiting-for-dust-to-settle.

The party ended after that and everybody left in a hurry.

This much is known about the rest of the night. Jamie and Marnie drove out to the Anchorman Arms on the other side of the lake where nobody much cared about the age of the patrons and everybody young and old got blind drunk. Near closing time, Pete, the barefoot owner, called out, "I'm going home. Everybody mark down how much more you drink."

People were basically honest. They poured doubles, charged themselves for singles, and Pete still made money.

Sam who had been at a friend's house on the reserve after the dance to share a couple of beers, started walking back toward town around two in the morning. Sometime after that, when the dirty little farm town bar had closed, a brawling drunk white shark of a car prowled the back roads out toward the highway. The air was heavy with the smell of sweetgrass. A thick fog rose from the bordering fields. Expensive tires hummed over concrete. When the shark rounded the corner, its headlight caught a dark figure walking in the direction of town. The shark sped up and the air filled with the sound of tires in the gravel chasing prey. A muffled thud hit the night.

A moment later all was quiet except for the chirrup of crickets and a soft rustling off the shoulder. The woods turned black as a cloud slid past the moon. At the edge of the ditch, the gentle head-smashed-in soul of Sam Crow danced a last slow dance. Three days later Sam was buried in the public part of the town cemetery.

The tire treads in the gravel matched those on Jamie's car, but three good ol' boys swore they'd been up all night with Jamie drinking whiskey and playing poker on the head of an oil drum in Gallagher's field. Some unknown driver must have stolen the car, taken it out for a joy ride, hit Sam, and brought the car back to the field before Jamie noticed it was gone. Charges were never laid. But Jamie did change his name to James after graduation. And he bought a print shop, so he learned to read upside down and mirror-wise, too. He always did have quick eyes.

Before Vanessa left town she visited Sam's grave. He was buried on a part of a hill so crowded with tombstones it looked like moraine rubble. She wove purple and yellow daisies into the stems of the wild carrot that grew up in the waste place beside the wooden cross that marked his spot. The image of a deer had been carved into the cross and a small fire had been lit nearby with the remains of a braid of sweetgrass laid in the ash. After her visit, she walked slowly down the hill and back toward her suite. Inside, she packed her clothing and books into two suitcases. When she walked out the door the final time she had a paint can stashed under her arm. She put the nearly empty can of midnight blue under the flattened cardboard in the drugstore dumpster.

KILLER BASS LINE

It happened during her seventh month at Amadea, the design shop Vanessa was lucky enough to land a job with in Victoria. It was the only good shop in the city at the time, unless you counted the shop run by the tailor in Oak Bay who wore half-glasses at the end of his nose and mostly produced heavy tweed fashions for seniors. She was fresh out of the George Brown Fashion program and incredibly happy to have made it to the West Coast—the place her stepfather liked to joke was where everything loose rolled "because the world's on a westward tilt".

Her mother was disappointed she'd even gone into fashion. "What can you do with a fashion diploma?" she'd asked. "All the way to Victoria," her stepfather had said. But the truth was, almost the minute Vanessa stepped off the plane, thoughts of returning to Toronto left her head.

She loved everything about Victoria. The fields strewn with pumpkins on the drive in from the airport, the sparkling water in the Inner Harbour, the exoticness of the tiny Chinatown that was also her new neighbourhood, her co-workers, Myra and Gary, her boss Amadea who lived in California and never bothered them, the logger Rob that she liked to get high with, and the cute fisherman Grant who was so much fun it didn't matter if he had a girlfriend in every cove up the coast. It was exciting to be out of Ontario and away from everything that she thought repressed her.

Then in that seventh month she met Jake, the bass player she consciously tried to build borders around, tried to fend off in her mind, but never could in her body. She knew his ego was out-sized and he had bad personal habits. But the thing she couldn't work around was the way he took her to bed. She wondered how much it had to do with his ability to snuggle into the bass like it was the most precious thing in the world. She wished she was music and he was in love with her.

They'd met in an incense shop in Fan Tan Alley—their hands glancing off one another as they both reached for the same package of sandalwood incense.

"What d'you need incense for?" he asked.

"To mask the smell of the kitty litter," she said.

"Well, as long as you don't keep the litter in the bedroom, I'm there."

They barely finished their mugs of tea at Murchies before she was leading him up the stairs to her flat above the vintage clothing shop on Pandora Street. She introduced him to her cat Shadow and her dress dummies, and they spent the next forty-eight hours tangled in a love-lock. It was a sweet time. He brought her tea in the evening when she was chilled, and when summer came and it warmed up, cold watermelon in the heat of the day. All the while she kept telling herself, Be careful, be careful, don't fall for this one. Despite the self-warnings, she let him take the next six months to move in.

The way he explained it, "I don't really have a home base. I work here, Vancouver, Seattle, Portland—wherever Roger Waters, Dee Dee Ramone or Charlie Haden isn't—I might as well make this my home, darlin', so I can see you when I'm here."

And see him she did, because he hardly ever wore clothing when they were alone in the flat. "I like to feel all parts of my body," he said. At first she thought it was funny, especially when it was cold and his balls shrank. But after a time she started to nag, tried to push him off the couch, make him sit on blankets, particularly when he needed a bath and he wanted to sit on her pale pink velveteen chair. Then finally it wasn't worth the struggle. Besides, the truth was she was addicted to the smell of him, even when he was in need of a clean. So, ultimately, she learned that to live peacefully with him was to put up with some exhibitionist bullshit and let it be.

She never believed Jake was going to be as famous as the bass players he liked to compare himself to, but a lot of musicians called, some with names like Grease, Shrew and Huge. So obviously he had work whenever he wanted it, even if too much of it was on cruises that took him away for weeks at a time, and after which he always brought back more stuff—Mexican maracas, Hawaiian ukuleles, and a strange Alaskan instrument made of caribou hide and a rusty hand saw.

She cleared the sewing supplies from the second bedroom, so he could make a music room, but in the end the entire flat was one big music mess. Scores, bows, cakes of rosin, keyboards, amplifiers—junk everywhere. He said he knew who he was, and she should step around his things, be grateful for the flirtation he let her have with the musical imagination. The time he came back from Catalina Island and presented her with a pretty turquoise scarf, he'd gone down on one knee and said, "The colour and pieces of space in the music, all of this I give to you." Afterward, they'd had hand-over-the-mouth-screaming sex, and she was mad at herself for getting hooked back in.

Then there were the actual basses themselves. He had what he called a quiver—six in all. At first they were stashed in various cities at friends' homes, but every time he went on tour he brought another one back. First to come was the expensive Italian acoustic. He played it at the high-class supper clubs and gala evenings, and carried a bow with it to use on the last note of ballads. He kept it in a case that doubled its size when it was so-called out of the way. Next was the rough standup with scratches over its body and strings high off the fingerboard. He thumped away on that one in the rockabilly bands. Then there was the fretted electric he took on the cruises, followed by the *avant garde* bass that looked more like a whale's rib mounted on a peg. The rib's sound was lousy, but its appearance was right for the crowd who liked what he called train wreck music. "It doesn't matter if the sound is no good, because those concerts usually have more members in the band than the audience," he said.

Then there was the bass Vanessa loved. The fretless electric, a beautiful aquamarine instrument that he always put clothes on to play. "This one takes the electric bass right out of being the bastard child of the acoustic," he said. The mistake she made around that bass was in trying to compliment him on its sound. She'd tried hard to learn everything she could about music and was proud she was beginning to distinguish one musician from another.

"You sound like that guy in Weather Report," she said.

Jake set the aqua instrument down. "Are you crazy? Jaco is great, but my style is my own. I'm more punk." Then he took a dramatic pause as if recovering from a terrible shock, and picked the bass back up, loosened a string, stuck a pick in it, and made a mean sound.

She couldn't help but laugh. He looked hilarious in the punk pose. Still she was confused when she found the album with Jaco's famous song 'Havona' hidden under a stack of tea towels in the linen cupboard. It was as if he didn't want people to know he even owned the record.

Finally there was the bass Vanessa came to hate. It was a knockoff Fender that he played in the punk bands who called way more often than she liked—once was too much. He got in an ugly mood whenever he played a punk gig. They had a huge argument the time he'd swung the bass around in the kitchen so violently he broke the creamer to the Willow Pattern tea set she'd brought all the way from Toronto.

"My grandmother gave me that when I was a kid," she admonished.

"Sorry, babe, that's the price you gotta pay. I need to be in a thrash mood to do this gig with Art. The mighty man does not call often."

Ever after she hated the faux Fender. Hated the people he played it with. Hated the way he left it propped up in the spare room, looking like the dark lord of destruction glowering in the corner. She tried to put one of her dress dummies in front of it, but Jake slung the guitar around the dummy's neck and anchored it to the wall. "So you can think of me when I'm gone," he said.

Myra at work thought Jake was a jerk. "You should pay attention to the subtle stuff," she started in one day. Vanessa had been standing captive in the middle of the lunch table at the back of the shop, while Myra pinned up the hem on a tulle dress they'd designed together. The dress was for a wealthy patron, a young woman who'd married an older titan of industry, but still fancied herself a bohemian. To make the point to her husband's tweed crowd, the woman had asked the shop to inset strips of doeskin into the bustier of the bodice.

"Like what subtle stuff?" Vanessa asked.

"Well I hate that crap he's always saying—'I'm an artist. I need to be free.' Get away." Myra looked up at Vanessa, her mouth full of pins.

"Ew," Gary chimed in from the corner. "I agree. Get away."

"How would you know, Gary?" Vanessa turned to look at him.

"I date guys, too. Or did you forget? I know an asshole when I see one."

"You do indeed, my friend." Myra laughed.

"How can you talk with your mouth full of pins, Myra?" Gary ribbed.

"Years of practice."

Gary threw a piece of tulle at them.

Mostly Vanessa put on a brave face about the whole *needing to be free* thing, but after the first year it was beginning to get to her how much time he was away. And even when he was in town, he had a million excuses for why she couldn't come to the shows with him. "The band rooms are stinky. Full of empty beer bottles. Club owners don't want girlfriends hanging around. The guys get uptight when they know people in the audience." The list was endless.

But the thing that started to hurt the most was the matter-of-fact delivery of his mantra. "I need space. Period." He always made a little circle with his forefinger when he said the word period. One time, he even tried to intellectualize it into some-thing that was supposed to be a positive. "The notes need space. To do that, I need space. I know the beats are there when I leave a space, just like I know you're there even when there's a space between us. It's a type of respect I'm showing you, babe."

She so much didn't feel the respect, she didn't know how to put it into words. All she could manage was, "I can't take you seriously. Put on some clothes."

"Yeah. Yeah. I'm getting dressed. I'm playing with the Lime Rickeys tonight, over at Harpo's. See ya later."

After he was gone, she sat on the couch with a sketchpad in her hand. She'd been working on some designs in her head that she wanted to sketch, but she couldn't draw properly. Her fingers felt cramped. She didn't like how love had shipwrecked her. Everything was going along fine until she met him. Then she fell, and all of a sudden life was hard, and she was alone.

Alone. Alone. Alone.

A mind-numbing word if she repeated it too often. A word she couldn't get out of her head when she tried to fall asleep at night. Tried not to need him, her stomach twisted into a knot, making her sick. For three nights she went to bed like this. On the third night, her stomach felt so strange she started to wonder if she had cancer. When he came home late, smelling of booze, and crawled into bed, he didn't even notice she was awake.

Next morning he didn't hear her in the bathroom throwing up. He was lying on his back gently snoring when she left for the day. By the time she got home from work, he was gone again on yet another cruise. She knew he was going, but his note was too plain. It simply said, "Back on the 27th possibly later." There was no hand drawn heart at the bottom, no *miss you* scrawled by his name, just the bare facts and not even that. The 27th of what month? It was the 2nd of July, with any luck he'd be back at the end of August, but maybe not until September.

That first week he was away, she couldn't eat anything but melba toast and stone wheat thins. Every time she went into the bathroom at the shop to throw up, she turned up the radio. She thought she was hiding it, until Myra, her mouth full of pins, again, looked up and said, "You're pregnant. Your bra size is bigger and you're throwing up all the time."

"I'm on the pill. I can't be pregnant. Besides Jake's hardly around enough to get me pregnant."

"When was your last period?"

"I dunno."

"Get a home test. First Blush is good. Two tests for the price of one, in case you goof the first try."

Vanessa wondered what Myra meant by goof the first try until she tried to pee into the tiny test tube that came with the kit. It was made for someone with a trickle no bigger than the outpouring of a parched mouse. On top of it there was the whole routine of carefully setting the tube in the miniature rack, then waiting thirty minutes without touching it, to see whether the ring at the bottom was blue.

And blue it was. No doubt about it.

When the results were official, the doctor said, "I hope it's what you want."

"No, it's not," she answered.

He opened his hands and said, "You can't wait long if you want to do something about it. You're already into the third month." He presented it as an option with no consequences, but available for only a limited time.

That night Vanessa refilled Shadow's water dish so often it overflowed and made a puddle in the centre of the kitchen linoleum. She stepped in the puddle without feeling the water and walked over a newly penned score Jake had left lying on the living room floor. The notes turned into a soft blur like an abstract Japanese watercolour. When she finally noticed what she'd done, she stooped to pick up the score and read the word he'd written in the corner. *Leitmotif.* She knew it meant a musical phrase that haunts, one that comes back on itself, again and again. Jake had told her, "On its second or third hearing the phrase begins to remind you of itself, so it's never really finished."

She began to wonder if she was living with a second or third unfinished version of him. Or was she the one who was unfinished?

She didn't tell anybody about the results. At night a new word crept into her head.

Abortion.

The word had to be repeated only once with intent to have the effect of an emotional lobotomy. By the time she returned to the doctor, she was so practised at feeling numb, it was easy to say what she needed.

"Have you thought this through?" the doctor asked.

"Yes," she lied.

"There's no going back," he said.

"I know."

General day surgery was a busy place. Patients were lined up all around the waiting room, some with limbs in splints, some with only socks on their feet, some with open wounds barely contained. Some, like Vanessa, who seemed apparently well.

"Do you have a ride home afterward?" the receptionist asked.

"Yes," she lied.

In pre-op, the pretty nurse covered to the eyeballs with a surgical mask, leaned in to ask, "Are you okay?"

"Oh, yes." She cried. The nurse held Vanessa's hand until she went under.

Afterward, she threw up in the taxi. She asked to get out a few streets early, so the driver could get to a clean-up station and she could breathe in some fresh air.

The Chinese grocer at the corner had cantaloupe melons on sale for 99 cents a pound. Most of the melons were overripe, and the small ones looked like babies' heads with the soft spots caved in. It made her woozy to look at them. In the empty flat, she crawled into bed and lay there like a wounded animal among Kleenex shreds and dog-eared magazines. She woke in the morning to the sound of a quiet boy's voice in her head. "Why did you do it, Mom?" he asked. She tried to answer. Tried to catch a glimpse of him before she was fully awake, but all that was left was a vision of curly golden hair and dark brown eyes, a bright light around his head. A lot like his father.

On the way to work, the stack of melons at the Chinese grocer's had been replaced with fresh ones. The price had gone up a dollar a pound.

Vanessa thought when she told Jake, he might be angry she hadn't waited. Dishonoured somehow that she hadn't talked to him about it. Possibly, even slightly disappointed things had been terminated. What she hadn't prepared for, was for him to be so uncaring, in the pure sense of seemingly not caring one way or another.

"Thanks for handling that, babe," he said. "Must have been a bit rough I wasn't around." Then maybe because he did feel a little sorry, he asked if she wanted to come to Harpo's that night to see a new band from Montreal. "Start of a new thing in music. Quite a buzz about them. Sort of punk, sort of not. Got a chick on bass."

Vanessa didn't like the sound of it, but didn't want him to go alone. Then when she saw the goddess on bass, she was horrified she'd ever thought it could in any way have been okay for her to have come with him. The voluptuous blonde was playing a knockoff, and Jake was behaving like the most inappropriate, lovesick groupie she'd ever heard him describe. He hung at the edge of the stage by the goddess, catcalling, or rather calling attention to himself, every chance he got. When the band finished its set, he came back to Vanessa at her bar seat and shouted, "Going to the band room. Amazing how she detuned and retuned on that D major riff."

He hadn't exactly told Vanessa not to follow him, though she knew she wasn't supposed to. By the time she got to the back hall, the room was already crowded, full of smoke and the sound of beer cans being opened. Jake pretty much filled the door in front of her, but she was able to see him reach over to shake the lead guitarist's hand, then not so much see as hear him turn to the goddess and say, "Killer bass line on that last number."

Vanessa saw a stiletto heel move off a chair, then open-legged fishnet stockings swivel full on around to Jake to say, "Well aren't you the cutie."

Vanessa watched her romance with Jake hit the beer-stained wall at the back of the band room right above the Echo & the Bunnymen poster. It was all she could do to stop herself from shouting into the cacophony, "I'm so inappropriate for him, even I can see it."

Then somehow in that moment it became mandatory for her to walk away. Not talk. Not look. Not think. Just walk.

See You Later Maybe Never

Jake puts his foot on the bed beside where Brian's tall frame sits hunched. He looks down at his lanky shoulders and asks, "Have you got your charts together for tonight?"

Brian squints up at him. "Course I do, man. Even though I so don't want to do this I piss blood."

"So that's what I see in the urinal after you've been in there." Jake doesn't make eye contact when he says this. Brian is a damn good musician and a rare find to have on a cruise, but Jake wants him to leave his cabin so he can catch some sleep.

Brian lets out a sigh and sits up straight, as if he's just remembered there's no bunk bed above him. Having a stateroom to himself is one of the perks Jake gets for being the musical director on the SS Prince Hawaiian. Brian has to bunk in with the drummer.

Jake peers through the tiny pinhole that's supposed to be his sea view.

"Finally. We're coming into Kona," he says. "The lounge will be packed tonight. Maybe we'll get some eye candy."

"With this crowd? Not a chance." Brian slaps the night table by the bed with the pent-up energy of a young man thwarted.

"You never know," Jake says. "Some rich guy's hot young wife might knock him out with a brandy and a hand job, so she can go on the prowl."

"Never, man. Be glad this isn't the nudist cruise. Ugliest bunch of cretins I've seen in a long time."

"At least since the last cruise you were on. Yeah? Okay Mr. Brian the Bone Goodman. Get outta here. Go limber up that trombone of yours. I got stuff to do."

Jake holds the door open for Brian and inhales the stench of the empty wine boxes stacked in the hall. When he took this job, he'd thought *own room* meant like a passenger, not some broom closet three levels down at the seasick end of the ship, right beside the kitchen garbage. It's the seventh week of his contract, and he's memorized the kitchen's routine by what's in the discard pile. Today is *demi-glace* day, gallons of cheap red wine boiled up with the bones left from the standing rib the night before. The hall stinks like a drunken dead man. A smell Jake is actually familiar with.

He strips off his clothes to lie on the bed and stare straight ahead. Really, even though the musicians have to pick Saran Wrap from the lounge chairs at the end of the evening, he likes the nudist cruises best. He wishes he was on one now. This trip—the badly named Sunset Jazz Cruise (most of what they're playing isn't even jazz)—has set new levels of boredom. The passenger music appreciation level is calibrated by the amount of energy remaining in the collective of hearing aid batteries assembled in the room. There's nothing like having a quiet bass solo drowned in the buzz of a dying battery while somebody's wife shouts, "Take out your hearing aids, Fred."

At least on the nudist cruise, the entertainment never ends. It's beyond bizarre watching naked people do everyday things like scope out the dinner buffet, play a game of shuffleboard, or learn to Watusi. Even Jake has to admit too many jiggling bits on the dance floor is reason enough to take the 'Limbo Song' and 'The Twist' out of the set list.

Eventually he gets off the bed and walks the two steps to his closet where he pulls jobbing suit number three from the rack. He wipes down the collar with a face cloth, removes what he can of the lint and dandruff, then carries the suit to the porthole to see what he's missed. Number three was new for this cruise, but the jacket is already shiny from where the bass rubs. He throws the jacket on the bed so he can survey the pants. They're shiny too from picking up his amp, moving it from room to room on the ship for the different gigs. Next time he signs on, if there is a next time, he's going to ask for a jobbing suit allowance. This is his shortest contract ever, but even at eight weeks the time at sea is taking a toll on more than just his suits. There's no chance for him to line up any kind of steady work for his own band. No chance even to find decent members for his band.

He's thirty-one years old, and he feels the pressure of time like a physical force on his back. No longer can he be the *enfant terrible* of the music world. The fact his career has taken up residence on a cruise ship might just mean he's a terrible musician. Period.

By the time Jake gets to the lounge, Brian's already there, noodling into the mic, checking the sound levels. His croon works well for the lounge, and his dance man stuff is perfect for the weekly show. He's turned out to be a great hire.

Skip, the drummer, is a different story. He arrives on the edge of being late every night and slides his stool in behind Jake. This night the metal leg of the stool catches the cuff on Jake's pant leg. They both hear the fabric tear.

"Damn," Skip says.

"Another notch," Jake mumbles.

Skip tries hard, but there can be a lot of crashing going on when things are meant to be quiet, and he doesn't get that a good drummer is supposed to follow the bass player's solo, not try to create his own on top of it. And for sure he doesn't get the pecking order of things. He has no hesitation in cutting Jake's lawn, especially when it comes to the ladies. Not that Jake is as into it as he used to be, or at least so he's pledged to Vanessa back home. Still, the contest over the ship's masseuse has left Skip and Jake bruised and pissed off with each other, despite both losing out to the dining room manager in the end.

Jake pulls a scratch of paper from his pocket. "Charts," he calls. "Okay in this order, 'In a Sentimental Mood, Night in Tunisia, Salt Peanuts, Perdido, Body & Soul, The Lady's a Tramp'…"

"For the rich guy's hot wife?" Brian interrupts.

Jake steps back in mock indignation. "May I resume, gentlemen?" He glances over at Skip. "And when she gets here, she's mine. You remember that, young fellow."

Skip flicks a brush on his snare, then uses it to salute. "Aye, aye captain. Sir!"

Jake holds the scratch that is the second set list, when Brian lets out a low wolf whistle—"She's here!" The three of them swivel to watch a statuesque all-American blonde wiggle her way across the lounge to take a seat at the bar.

Jake grabs his bass and makes a hot thumb sound on it and does a bit of a body hump before reading the chart list. When he's finished, Brian pipes up. "No '*Voulez-Vous Coucher Avec Moi*' this set?"

"Who said that wouldn't be happening?" Skip laughs.

Jake is aware the blonde is boring holes into his back while he plays through the set. Every time he bends to adjust his amp, he sneaks a look. She is unabashed.

Once the set is done, he heads to the bar to order a soda water. He wants something stiffer, but staff's not allowed to drink alcohol in the passenger lounge. The bartender, a friend, pushes his glass further down the bar than is necessary, but Jake doesn't have to make a move. The blonde does it for him.

"What was that last number?" she asks, her lips pouting just enough.

He lowers the soda from his mouth. "'It Don't Mean a Thing'."

"If it ain't got that swing. Right? I like that. Though not everything has to mean something."

"Absolutely. A lot of things don't mean anything at all."

It turns out to be way too easy for Jake to sleep with her. She's gorgeous, she's into him, she's on the ship for only one night to cruise to Maui (she knows somebody who knows somebody), and importantly, he won't have to see her again on the decks and pretend to still be into her when he isn't. Except, as she's readying to leave the next morning, he is still into her. It hurts when he asks for her name and she says, "You don't need to know, Xavier. Call me Charo. This was fun. Let's keep it that way."

When she clutches her handbag and swivels through the door, Jake follows. Before she disappears into the throng at disembarkation, she turns and says, "See you later maybe never." He's left standing at the bottom of the gangplank waving to nobody.

Back in his cabin, he takes off his clothes to lie on the bed and puzzle over what has just happened. This is a short contract, he'll be back home in Victoria before his body barely realizes he's left. So why had he done it? Even more, why does the thought of returning to Vanessa give him such a sinking feeling? He'd had high hopes when he left the last time that he'd weather through this contract as a faithful partner, behave like someone approaching adulthood. Why is it unraveling, again?

He suspects it has a lot to do with the look Vanessa has started to give him whenever he leaves the apartment, even if it's only to go around the corner to buy a quart of milk. A look of such disappointment, it cuts to his centre. It says he's a bad person. Makes him wonder, Why do I even bother to try?

He should be practiced at the look. He's been getting it for years from his mother. The first time he can remember it, all he'd done was ask his mother if he could go on an overnight to Fredericton with his high school band mates. They'd been hired to play a gig. A real gig, with travel expenses and a hundred bucks. It wasn't like he'd asked if he could go across the country. He remembers wheedling. "Fredericton isn't even two hours from Saint John. How can you stop me?" Still a part of him knew it was too soon. He should have waited.

His mother had been sitting amongst the jumble of half-finished afghans and quilts that seemed to be all that was left of her life, her hand clasped around a can of beer. She had a look of such distress when she spoke, and said, "If you go, Jacob, you'll forever be my fallen angel."

But he owned one of the first Stooges' albums, Iggy Pop was his idol, and he was destined to become a great rocker too. So nothing, not even fallen angels and Lucifer himself, was going to get in the way of his going to that gig in Fredericton. Still it nearly broke him when he walked out the front door, and his mother had come at him with one of her quilts, tried to put it around his shoulders. "You need it to keep warm," she'd said. "They should have covered your Dad up. They shouldn't have let him lie in the cold like that. Please, son. Cover up. Don't let anything happen to you."

His mother was the fallen angel.

There's that about Vanessa, too. Who knew when she told him that afternoon over tea at Murchie's that she was a fashion designer, that it really meant she lived like his mother, surrounded by mismatched swatches of fabric and unfinished sewing projects. He thought fashion designer meant artist, not crazy quilt maker. He needs the artist in Vanessa to come out, not the leader of the ladies' sewing circle. Not someone who spends time memorizing the names of famous bass players so she can fumble her way through conversations about music with him. Not someone who tries to inhabit him by attempting to play the badly-tuned ukulele he'd left at her apartment. And oh god, the time she'd followed him into the band room at the Town Pump, and sat in the corner plunking and singing with that awful tremulous treble of hers. She'd sounded worse than Tiny Tim. So dreadful, he'd had to ban her from coming to gigs with him.

Jake is dizzy with the need for sleep. Before he passes out, he flips through his Fake Book to be sure he's got everything he needs for the upcoming evening. Only one more week of this, he thinks, as he drops the book on the floor.

Final night on the cruise is always a Club night, which means the full eight-piece band is on hand to politely contend with a lot of goofy requests and pretend to play their hearts out on numbers like 'Celebrate', 'Shake Your Booty' and 'Freak Out'. After the band plays 'Y.M.C.A.' for the second time, the waiter who doubles as the dancer with the Indian headdress having finally shown up, Jake turns to Skip and says, "Okay, we're going to wrap up the musical end of things for this cruise with 'Wipe Out'."

Skip, whose forehead is already slick as a big-old piece of deli meat left on the table too long, makes an audible groan. But he gamely picks up his sticks and plays enough of a surfer riff on the tom to send his band mates scrambling for the chart. When Jake feels a collective readiness, he counts, "One, and two, and you guys screw… uh, uh, uh." After a couple of notes, the spry old guys are out on the floor jumping like surf's up and they're wearing new surfer jams. Most everybody who joins in looks as if they're about to break a hip. Still it's a good vibe, and a cheer goes up when Brian shouts, "Wipe Out!" and leaps from the stage onto the dance floor to begin an oddly sexual dance that includes a full body shake every time Skip crashes a cymbal.

Jake likes ending the cruise this way. There's not a lot for the bass to do on the number, so he doesn't have to contend with the over-busy keyboardist who's playing attack bass with his foot anyway.

When the song ends, Jake turns to Skip and says, "Nice work with the high hat chick on two and four. You got it all going on tonight."

Skip looks pleased and later, in the staff lounge, he asks Jake, "Can I spot you a drink? It's been good working with you."

Jake, who is already into his third beer and feeling some of the early fuzzy high of cruising into homeport, turns. "No, I insist. What can I get you?"

"Ginger ale."

"That's right. You don't drink. Good on you. You'd be a match for my girlfriend, Vanessa. She doesn't drink much either."

"You have a girlfriend?" Skip's face sets in a look of genuine surprise.

"Yeah. Kinda have to feel for her, don't you?"

"Sort of. I mean, you know. Sorry. Don't mean to offend."

"It's okay. I get it."

By the time Jake is finished his fourth beer, he's contemplating what it might be like to set Vanessa up with Skip. He's not sure whether it's the alcohol or having found a solution to his problem that makes him feel relieved, but when he's standing talking to Brian his head is in the mindset of a single man who has nothing on his brain but music.

"Tell me, Brian the Bone, who are those musicians that piss blood?"

Brian leans back as if what he's about to say might smell bad, or cause Jake to do something physical. He makes a motion with his arm like he's throwing a football. "'Cause they haven't been able to keep their art underneath their arm while they go rushing into the end zone," he says.

"They fumble?"

"No. The ones who piss blood are too good to fumble, but they've let a bunch of losers get in their way. You can't get into the zone with lightweights on your team."

Jake looks at Brian. "Maybe I'm a loser."

"You will be if you don't get off this cruise gig. You gotta form your own band, put a tour together. Me, I'm done with pissing blood. I'm headed to New York next. No more cruises. Time to get serious."

"Yeah but these cruises, they pay. And if we stop in port in LA, we can cruise the Strip. Check out the scene at The Roxy and Whiskeys."

"After you've been to those clubs you've been to them. You should be playing them."

"For a kid, you're pretty smart."

"Street smart. Personally, I think your university music fucked you up, man. That MusBac is only good for teaching high school and being the boss on a cruise ship. You lost your roots. My advice is do one thing awesomely."

"Awesomely. Absolutely." Jake looks down at his feet. "I think I see a little Dee Dee Ramone sprouting from my big toe."

They found Jake's father's body frozen to the floor in the bandshell at King's Square Park in Saint John. Nobody knew where he'd been earlier in the evening, or how long he'd been there, but probably most of the night, after he'd been kicked out of some pub or other. At first the authorities refused to bring him home, said the body had to go to the morgue and from there to a funeral parlour or burial. But Jake's mother went crazy on them. She screamed it was her family's custom to have a viewing in the front room, and it was her right to have it. She'd get a court order if necessary.

They brought his father's body back embalmed inside a closed casket and left it on the living room floor where it sat for a week like a beacon of doom. When the authorities returned to get him the final time, his mother was so collapsed with fatigue and drink she no longer had the strength to argue with them.

Jake knew it didn't make sense that he could smell his father inside the casket, but he swore he could. The musty fermented stink of death by alcohol permeated his nostrils long after the casket was removed. He could still smell it months later when he asked to go to Fredericton. It wasn't right to be seventeen years old and to spend all your time with your mother. The stench of his dead father remained, so did the look of disappointment in his mother's eyes.

While he stands at the closed door to Vanessa's apartment in Victoria on Pandora Street, before he puts the key in the lock, he can see that disappointed look in her eyes. He feels like a bee trapped inside a mason jar, banging up against the walls of his history. He inhales a big breath, lets it out, and raps on the door instead of unlocking it. As the door opens, he knows whatever is about to come out of his mouth will be wrong. It will hurt. He will fail.

"Hey, Vanessa."

"Hey, Jake. You're back. Nice to see you."

"You too. How's things?"

It feels so awkward, and after she blurts, "I had an abortion," the field in front of him is suddenly littered with fallen angels. He makes an involuntary grip of his arm muscle, like somebody might steal the art right out from under him, and he wants to cry because he is becoming his father, and that can't happen or he will die frozen to the bandstand full of trampled dreams like his dad, so instead of letting himself go there, he makes a muddle of it. "Oh jeez. Thanks for handling that. Must have been rough on your own."

Then she is talking, a lot of words. He can see her mouth moving, but most of it he can't hear because the cycle of family is backed up into his head.

After a time, when the roaring in his mind starts to clear, he does hear her say, "It's okay. You're right, I handled it. It feels good to be able to tell someone, though." And then because he needs to believe she is okay with it in order for him to keep on standing in the room, to not bolt out the door and run all the way back to Saint John to beg for his mother's forgiveness, which he knows if he does will mean he'll never play another note of music again, and he'll get so sucked back into the never-ending black hole that is his mother's life, it will become his black hole, too, and because he desperately needs for this not to happen, he keeps standing exactly in the same position until a part of him really does believe Vanessa has handled it, that she really is okay with it, despite him not being clear on what procreation that ends in an abortion even entails, all of it too huge and godlike for him to consider: so to take it out of this place of fallen angels and into the church of his art, he hears himself say, "Do you want to come see a band at Harpo's with me tonight?" He says this despite knowing he's on his way to the club with the hope that something meaner and tougher is there waiting for him.

He holds his breath, hoping against hope Vanessa will say no. But fallen angels never do as they should. As she walks closer to the door, readying to leave with him, pulling on the cherry-coloured jacket she made herself, the one with too much padding in the shoulders, Jake feels a sudden unscrewing of the lid on the Mason jar. The hermetic seal around the relationship pops. She moves forward for a kiss, but he is already hurtling down the field toward the end zone leaping over fallen bodies that aren't able to see who it is that's flying above them. He pushes out the door ahead of her, and her lumpy shoulders, because there's barely any time left.

ENCHANTED GIRL

Tall and tan and young and lovely
~ 'Girl from Ipanema', Antonio Carlos Jobim

Fairies whirl around Vanessa's face and land on her shoulders. Astrud Gilberto's voice floats from the transistor radio propped on the hood of her stepfather's new Mustang. Afternoon sun filters into the garage catching specks in the air from Vanessa's sweeping behind the garbage bins. And the family's debris turns to golden fairy dust, just like in 'Midsummer Night's Dream'.

Her grade ten class had studied the play that year and Vanessa had loved it, though she wasn't exactly sure what was going on all the time. Even for Shakespeare, she makes up her own subtext. She wonders now if the sprite Puck used juice or pollen from the love-in-idleness flower to cast his spells. She thinks briefly about going inside to dig through the jumble in her cupboard to find the notes she'd made of what the teacher had said about it. But she can't be bothered and decides it must have been pollen. She sweeps again and closes her eyes to let love land on her eyelids.

Tall and tan and young and lovely.

She is not tall, but then neither are Brazilians by North American standards. She's pretty sure about this. She looks down at her arms. They're tanned, but barely. It's taken a whole summer of broiling in the backyard slathered in a mixture of Johnson's baby oil and iodine to achieve the meager result. Not to mention the ordeal of listening to her mother. "You're going to be more wrinkled than I am if you're not careful. Come inside now, Vanessa."

Today, despite not being tall and having a barely-there tan, she is lovely. Hadn't the boy who drives the red Volkswagen bus

by the tennis courts said so? Isn't "hey girl, lookin' fine" as close
to lovely as it's going to get from a skateboarding dreamer boy?
And so what if her girlfriends say he's only looking to pick up
anybody who will share the cost of a drive to California. The way
he watches her is different. He even knows her name, called her
over to his bus and said, "Vanessa, you sure would look gooo-
ood in a bikini on Ocean Beach."

When she'd asked around, the stories she'd heard were
beyond exciting. He's seventeen, and he's two grades ahead of
her, though her friend Linda heard he dropped out before finals
because he's moving back to San Francisco to live with his father,
who is either an actor or a plumber, or possibly both. Then Kitty
told her his name is Dylan, and he's a good kisser, but he's more
likely eighteen, or possibly even nineteen, because they put him
back a grade when he moved to Canada. Kitty knows more than
Linda because her older sister, Liz, dated Dylan for a while. She
thinks Liz is still "into him" despite his having stopped talking to
her the day after he left her neck covered in hickeys.

All of this is cool, except Vanessa doesn't like to remember
how Kitty reacted when she admitted to having a crush on him.
"You're an idiot if you fall for Dylan. He's out of your league.
Even Liz couldn't hang on." For a moment Vanessa believed
Kitty. She can be a nerd. She likes to stay home and fool around
with Simplicity sewing patterns in the basement. Sometimes she
even designs her own clothes on her mother's Singer and wears
the outfits to school, though she hates it when people say, "You
made that yourself, didn't you?" Still, it's okay, at least she's
doing something for herself and that makes her strong. She's
pretty sure about this, too.

And it's all part of the attraction, that there are others and he
continues to like her better. Especially when she puts it together
with the story Jane told her about him playing guitar in a Bay
area band that's probably going to be the next Buffalo
Springfield. "They're waiting to release their first album, and
that's why he has to get back to California," Jane said. It all makes
sense to Vanessa. She swivels her hips around the broom while
Astrud sings.

When she walks, she's like a samba.

She presses the handle of the broom into her body thinking about Dylan's tanned chest and arms. He's more filled out than the other boys at school, and her body responds in a curious lush way to the hard angle of the broom. It's a new feeling. Sort of scary, but thrilling at the same time. She pushes the broom forward to make the fairy dust swirl to the crown of her head again. The future gleams in front of her like the polished point of an opal. She has become an enchanted girl.

A girl who can put her broom down and walk out of the garage all the way to Haight-Ashbury like her Aunt Marion did. A girl who can reinvent herself, write dangerous music like Grace Slick, smoke black cigarettes like Joni Mitchell, and design flowers around any prairie dress Laura Ashley might create. A girl who could even suck off Jim Morrison, if he hadn't died four years ago already, and she had any clue what sucking off really means.

She pulls the broom back into herself and kisses it, opening her mouth like she'd seen Julie Christie do in the movie 'Darling'. She sweeps the dirt into a corner behind the side door, and with a mix of fairy dust, dead rock stars, and a red Volkswagen bus in her head, walks out of the garage, down the driveway and toward the tennis courts.

A block in, she wonders if her homemade, ribbed tube-top is right for where she's headed. She has no bra on underneath it. But Dylan would respect her. He wouldn't venture beneath on their first time. She wishes she was more sure about this.

As she approaches the tennis courts, she starts to wish she'd put on some lipstick, maybe some of the strawberry-flavoured gloss her mom gave for her birthday. She imagines Dylan tasting it, licking his lips at the pleasure of it.

At the courts she waits. And waits.

Eventually she sees his VW bus drive down the street toward her. Thoughts of what she is or is not wearing fly out of her head.

The bus stops at the edge of the field. She stoops to pick a daisy from a clump growing there, and offers it to Dylan as she steps up into the seat. His bus smells of marijuana and patchouli oil, a smell she knows from Kitty's house, from the time Liz had her friends over, and they'd sat in the backyard toking and getting goofy, until they all left to party somewhere with alcohol. Vanessa and Kitty were too young to follow, so they had to stay behind and clean up the mess before the parents came home.

Dylan takes the daisy from her and puts it behind her ear. "There," he says, "like a real California girl."

He pushes in the clutch and with a roar the bus heads toward the high school. The main parking lot is empty because school doesn't start for another week. He keeps going and parks in the secluded, service lot behind the football field, and kills the engine. He turns to ask, "You from around here?"

The question surprises her. She thought he knew they went to the same school.

"I'm from Islington," she says.

"Where in hell's name is that?"

"Here," she says, pointing down between her legs. As she points, she realizes how stupid it looks.

"This," he says pointing to his own crotch, "is Etobicoke."

"You're right." She smiles. "It's just that my grandmother used to correct me when I said Etobicoke. She thought Islington sounded better. It's what they once called this place." She rotates her finger trying to bring in the strength and wisdom of old Islington to guide her through this first encounter with what she now realizes is a real man. Not a boy. Not like Greg who sat behind her in English class hopelessly in love with her nerdy fashions and strawberry lip gloss.

"Do you always do what your granny says?" He leans forward and removes her tube top with one smooth motion of his hand up and over her head.

"No." Vanessa giggles, even though she doesn't feel like laughing. He hadn't asked if it was okay—and the way he'd done it—sort of pulled the top off and threw it in the back as if he were flicking a tea towel.

"I like the halter you wore for me," he says. He moves in to kiss a nipple.

Part of her wants to protest except the kissing feels okay, in an unexpectedly gooo-ood way. Still she's uncomfortable, worried that one of the boys fooling around on the football field might see them. So she tries to push his head away, change the mood.

"I hear you're going to San Francisco," she says. "Want some company?"

"Come on," he says, "you got me all worked up here."

His hand moves toward the drawstring on his jam shorts and soon he's exposed, urging her head down toward him.

She wasn't down very long and doesn't even know what it is she did to make the warm spurt of liquid that hits her cheek, but when it's over he seems happy enough. No sooner has he cleaned up the puddle in his pubic hair, licking his fingers as he goes, than he fires up the bus and heads back toward the tennis courts. She has to reach behind the seat to find her top and pull it back on while they drive.

When she descends from her seat, the daisy she'd given him falls to the pavement. He drives over it with a "see you" as he leaves. She watches the bumper with the peace sticker disappear. She stands and thinks how he hadn't asked if she wanted a drive home. Maybe that's the way more experienced people do it. Besides it's not that big a deal sucking someone off. Next time he might even take her up on her offer to drive to California with him. Or maybe she'll go by herself. The possibilities are still endless, just not quite as gleaming as before.

Her mother waits for her in the garage. The sun filtering through the open door is no longer golden, it's more a burnt orange.

"You walked out of here," her mother says, "without putting the lid on the can. The dog threw garbage everywhere. Look. Behind the door. See the pile of dirt you swept there. Do you see?"

But she doesn't see. She just doesn't see.

She wonders how to live an enchanted life when the golden fairy dust has burned to orange.

— PART THREE —

LATER

HUNTING SEASON

Tom has been by again. Vanessa can tell by the plop of salsa on the flagstone patio. He always leaves something behind, an elbow smudge on the sliding glass door, a hand smear on the garden table, a fingerprint on the patio dimmer switch. He can't help it if his body gives off so much heat it leaves grease traces everywhere, but why would he bring a burrito, or calzone, or whatever overstuffed fast-food thing it was he'd been munching on, to her space? Not having to clean up after someone else is supposed to be one of the perks of living on her own.

It's been more than a year since Vanessa closed on the deal to buy Tom out of their house. Still, he behaves like a confused dog returning to its *spot* on the porch. Surely he doesn't want to revisit the incident when she'd nearly clobbered him with the meat-tenderizing hammer. But he'd never worn a hat before in the city, not even on the coldest day. So why had he worn one that first time he came back uninvited to sit? All she could see was the top of a stranger's hat on her patio, so she'd grabbed the hammer as she went to the door to investigate. Had Tom believed the hat made him invisible? And why, when he'd asked if she'd thought about calling the police instead of almost bludgeoning him, hadn't she simply told him the truth?—because somehow I knew it was you, but you looked stupid in that hat. And then his excuse for being there—because I miss the evening light and I just wanted to sit in the yard. All that had done was make her feel like a mean, unhinged shrew.

The kicker is that Tom has only moved up the street from the house, to the Garden Court apartments. And he never told her he was renting the corner suite, the one where he can watch from his living room window whenever her car drives by. To say nothing about him knowing her favourite shortcut walking route to Bayview is through the courtyard, passing right beneath his bedroom window.

This is what upsets her the most. Especially when she still has dreams she will meet a man and bring him home through the courtyard after pizza at Vero's restaurant. Maybe let the man stay the weekend if he's so inclined, though it feels like it's never going to happen that she will eat pizza with a man at Vero's. All she ever meets are women, more women, and the odd man in a writing workshop who puts new meaning into the word odd.

Now she only gets to observe men—sitting hungover at Starbucks staring into the dregs of an Americano, shuffling the aisles of the Valu-Mart searching for discount meats—most looking like they could have given themselves a better shave or worn a more decent pair of shoes.

All in all at this point, she is prepared for Tom to come by now and again, secretly sometimes likes it. It's just that she wishes he hadn't chosen today of all days to do it. His presence has sullied the ground of her creative nest, all but physically pricked the pity sanctuary she's been working on since she received the email earlier in the day from the obscure literary journal 'The New Orillian'.

The promise of her first publication should have been a thrill. And it was for a second, but too quickly it put her into a funk about the lateness of it all, the confirmation that she could have been a contender if only she'd gotten down to it sooner. If only she'd started to write before she was nearly sixty. It's too late now for her to be the *wunderkind* of any publishing house, not even a little-known house noted for its difficult to understand works.

Just the same, the acceptance of her poem 'Spring Breakup', the poem she honed into an extended metaphor mapping the dissolution of her marriage, boosted the imaginative forces that whirled in her head enough for her pick up a pen and spill out a few new lines: *some museum works of art remind of you/ surrounded by hospital whiteness/ standing alone from all the rest/ sad and sometimes sickening/ sick in colour/ sad in spirit/ museum works nonetheless.*

These lines have nothing to do with Tom. And she doesn't want him anywhere near them. Yet she's kicking herself because she knows in a way it's her fault he's come by. Starting a poem she's been mulling over for half a lifetime had been exhausting, so too soon into it she'd headed up to Bayview for a cappuccino. But she shouldn't have cut through the Garden Court courtyard. And she shouldn't have gone around under Tom's bedroom window to sneak a peek. She knew she was tempting fate, but she needed to figure out the essence of her poem, and to do that she told herself she needed to drink in the blood red of the begonia's growing beneath Tom's window. Afterward, when she'd looked up to the golden maple in the centre of the courtyard, the contrasting colours had fused a feeling to the front of her brain. That feeling, she's certain, is what kicked off the rest of the afternoon's events.

She'd gone to Starbucks. While she waited to order a cappuccino, she watched the two baristas so busy flirting they couldn't get the customers' drinks out in any timely way. She pondered why it is that women always fall for the bad ones. She briefly thought about warning the plump barista with the badly dyed, purple hair that her thin, attractive workmate with the expensive haircut was merely entertaining himself through his shift. He had no intention of ever getting back to her seriously. But when the two of them eventually produced a cup of milky, separated cappuccino for her, she let it go, only mouthed the words "thank you", and hit the sidewalk to catch the afternoon sun.

That's when she saw the boy. He came running straight at her, sun bouncing off his golden curls, a shining red halo behind him. Brightness obscured his face and for a moment he could have been any boy, anybody's boy. Her boy. The same boy who came running after her in the dream so many years before, to ask, "Why did you do it, Mom?" So strange to hear her child speak only once, and then only in a dream after she had literally shattered him.

She stumbled at the sharp pain of the memory and banged into the young mother standing beside the boy. "Forgive me," she said.

"No problem," the young woman answered.

Vanessa almost said, "Not you. I'm sorry to the boy." But she pulled it together and kept moving. As she walked, another line came to her—*forgive me the glass womb you were consigned*—she stopped to scribble it down on the back of her Starbucks' receipt. It was a good one; still, as she wrote, she wondered whether she could use it. Had she made it up, or had she heard it or read it somewhere else? This happened often. All the good lines felt like they belonged to someone else. But she at least knew then that the poem was about the boy himself not his father.

She took the long way home and for the rest of the walk golden boys were all she could see. In strollers, in the arms of happy mothers, running free in the park.

So, melancholy is the mood she's in when she spots the salsa on the flagstone. She sits at the patio table in a semi-stunned space, staring down at the splat, and hears the sound of the latch on the side yard gate opening. Knowing that Tom has already been by, he should be the last person she expects, but she knows it's him before she turns to look.

"It's such a warm fall day, Tom. Why are you wearing a hat again?" she asks.

"I take it you don't like the hat."

"Not especially."

Tom stands beside her and looks at the plop of red food near her foot. "Sorry," he says. "I'll clean that off."

He uncoils the hose on the back wall and begins to spray cold water at the salsa, some of it splashing at Vanessa's ankles. After he's rewound the hose, he sits with her.

"Came by to get my duck hunting equipment," he says. "You weren't here before."

She says nothing. She knew when she agreed he could keep his equipment in the basement, it would mean the duck hunting disarray would never leave, would remain a portal for him to get back into her life. Now that he's here looking for it again, she wishes she'd insisted it be gone. This breaking up but living nearby and sharing access to space in the house is confusing.

"Do you mind if I go inside to get it?" he asks.

"Seems too early in the year for hunting," she says.

"First day of the season. Tomorrow."

"Really?"

"So?"

"So? What?"

"Do you mind?"

"Mind what?"

"Hey, what's eating you, Vanessa? You seem very distracted."

"I am."

The two of them sit for a time. This is the same place they've been to many times over the years of their marriage. A place where one or both of them starts out with a specific quest for information or understanding, and the other simply drifts into a knot of misunderstanding, miscuing, and sometimes simply miss-caring. They get lost in the emotion, and neither bothers to look for the breadcrumbs to find a way out.

In a moment of needing to get going, or perhaps simply of wanting to leave because the sun is finally starting to set, Tom asks again in a more personal way. "What's wrong? You seem unhappy."

"I am. There's someone I'm thinking about. Someone who I've thought about a lot over the years. But not for a while. Someone I need to say I'm sorry to, but can't."

Tom sits up straighter in his chair and scratches at his temple. The motion tilts his hat a touch, and Vanessa can see a corner of white underneath. White that looks like a bandage. She decides to say nothing, but wonders if maybe Tom got in a fight. That seems so uncharacteristic, but what else could have happened to his head?

"I guess that person is not someone you want to talk about," Tom says.

"Maybe I should. I never told you."

She watches as Tom's hand goes toward his head again as if to itch, but he thinks the better of it and lets the hand settle in his lap. She knows he probably believes she's about to tell him something about another man, and she isn't sure how to start, so she starts with the other man.

"Well you know about that fellow Jake in Victoria. The bass player."

"Yeah. The guy the world was going to hear about, but never did. I know about that guy."

"What I didn't tell you is that I got pregnant with him."

"Oh. You have a child somewhere?" It seems to Vanessa that Tom is smiling. She's pretty sure the notion of a child somewhere is appealing to him. This adds a layer of confusion she hadn't contemplated.

"No. Sometimes I wish I did. But I terminated the baby. This is a hard word for me to say. Baby. I haven't told many people this story, including myself really. I don't usually think of him as a baby, in my head he's mostly just an it, and for a long time I didn't know whether I missed it simply because I wanted to be like everyone else and have a baby—you know me, need to keep up with the neighbours—but I had a dream once when he came and spoke to me. So I know he's not an it. I've known for years, but for some reason I am, today, totally confused about him. Today I feel like I need to say I'm sorry. But there's no one to say the words to. And that makes me sad."

She stops. She knows, and probably Tom does, too, that other than readings at her writing workshops, this is the most number of words she has said to anyone in a couple of years. In the quiet, she realizes how little emotion she usually lets herself feel and that whatever amount she does have, she's been parsing out for years like there's a limited supply.

"You can say sorry to me," Tom says, "and I can try to use my energy with you to pass the message on to the boy."

Vanessa sits back in her chair. She realizes there is little chance anyone could have said it better than Tom, starting with, 'The guy the world was going to hear about, but never did.' But she's afraid she might start to cry if she speaks now. She looks up. Trails of gathering darkness shimmer like delicate pulses. The sky is organic, parts of it like a baby's veined hand struggling in the cocoon of night.

The two of them could have remained in silence for quite some time except that the next-door neighbour begins to fuss with his garbage bins, then brings out his leaf blower to tease out the autumn detritus caught along the edge of the fence.

"What did the boy say?" Tom asks, raising his voice enough to be heard.

"He asked me why I'd done it."

"And?"

"I didn't have an answer for him. I had nothing to say. For a while, I was so messed up, I even contemplated joining a nunnery. That is, until I really looked into it. No way I could take four prayers a night. Besides it wouldn't have fixed anything. I've never shaken the feeling there's something I need to make amends for."

"You know, none of this changes the way I think about you."

"Thank you, Tom. Some people would think the worse of me for what I did."

"Nothing to thank. It's okay the way it is."

"I've been thinking, though." Vanessa has to raise her voice to be heard over the advancing leaf blower, and Tom rubs his forehead, which cocks his hat further back, as if to ask, What next?

"I've been thinking that maybe I should have a burial for the baby."

Tom doesn't say anything.

"It would make me feel better," she says.

The neighbour turns off the leaf blower and Vanessa says the word better in too loud a voice.

"Okay," Tom says softly.

At this, she turns to look at him straight on and grabs his arm. "What happened to your head?"

"This," he says, adjusting his hat. "It's nothing. A bit of work I had done."

"A bit. It looks like a lot."

What she can see of Tom's mostly baldhead is crisscrossed with fine black stitches. One wound toward the front is seeping and has the white bandage over it.

"The round last year, they went a touch too gentle on me. They had to go deeper this time. But it's nothing, really. They got it all."

Vanessa is surprised how much this upsets her. How on the edge she feels with so many of her emotions. Invincible Tom has been cut. As she looks at him, there's a thought in her mind she can't say—Nice guys take a lifetime to appreciate. She doesn't believe she's earned the right to say this yet. And she isn't sure what it would really mean if she did say it. Still, she appreciates the impish grin he's giving her.

Perhaps it's the length of the silence between them that compels Tom to go back a topic or two in their conversation.

"You know what they say about the first day of hunting season?"

"No. What?"

"They say, it's the day you settle your scores. Could be you need to do a little settling, lady."

"Okay. But first tell me something. Why are you here? With me? I was nasty. I apologize for that."

"Maybe I'm supposed to be here to watch what happens. Watch the relationship."

"Come inside," she says, rising from her chair. "You can get your hunting equipment. And I need to find something upstairs."

While Tom is in the basement, Vanessa is in her bedroom searching the drawers of her bureau. She's looking for the dahlia tuber that's like a tiny human with the *Allium Schubertii* head. When she finds the dried onion flower with explosive golden hair, she removes the porcupine quill she'd plunged into the side of the tuber when she'd believed it was nothing more than a voodoo of Jake, the father of the golden boy. The tuber is both the father and the son. She feels real pain as she withdraws the quill and understands even more deeply the connection between her body and the body of the baby she devastated. She picks up the paper with the line of poetry on it that she's been keeping in the drawer beside the tuber. *The moon hangs like a bruised plum in the sky/how dare he do this to me.* She rewrites the last line to say *how dare he do this to us/ perhaps he didn't know any better.* The line had been about Jake and was meant to be written into a poem. It's no longer simply that, it's a lament about Jake that belongs with the body of their baby. She wraps the tuber in the paper with the onion flower sticking out of the top, then walks across the hall into the bathroom. Under the harsh, fluorescent makeup light, she snips a piece of her hair to add.

When she joins Tom in the yard, he already has the shovel. She holds the tiny dahlia tuber in her hand and together they walk toward the plum tree. Tom clears away some fallen leaves. He hands her the shovel to dig. Vanessa thinks, only with Tom could I have come to this place. Somewhere in this, there might be a joinder of sorts. She digs one layer deeper than she really needs to, before she lays the body into the small grave. She knows the words on the paper are not really accurate, but at least they evoke some essence of the father, and her golden boy will not go down alone.

"Peace, little soul," she says.

She drops soil onto him, pats the dirt, and crouches by the spot to place her hand over it. She is willing the tuber to grow into a beautiful orange dahlia. For a second she believes it will, and that she is still an enchanted girl.

LOVE STRAIGHT, NO CHASER

Tom knows he's lucky he got a ground floor suite in the Garden Court where he's lived for two years since breaking up with Vanessa. He likes to tell people, "It has its own entrance. It's almost a townhouse but at an apartment price." Four three-storey brick buildings are arranged like a child's building blocks around a central courtyard. The manager, a middle-aged, red-haired man named Bruno, told Tom the City of Toronto wants to get its hands on the property, tear the buildings down and make a park. "Some consider them low class in a fancy part of town," Bruno said. "But the owner, Dr. Kapatis, he's stubborn and hangs on. Good for me. I get to keep my job."

Tom is grateful to be able to walk out his front door and not worry about having to see the others who live in the building. Most of them are old. Not the groovy kind of old he will be, but pensioners with the colour drained from their cheeks, some a sickly-grey autumn pallor, a few suffused with the shades of alcoholism. They at least look like they get some kind of kick out of life.

He believes the only reason he got into the building is because he walks upright, and looks young in comparison to the general pack of renters—thank God for his years on the basketball court and good genes. Once a person gets a suite in the Garden Court, they don't usually leave until they go out feet first.

Bruno confided, "I've had to escort more than my share out on their last legs. Dr. Kapatis asked me to stop renting to old people. But I like them." It helps Tom to know Bruno believes he's young enough to share this confidence.

Despite having turned sixty-eight, Tom feels young and hates reminders of where age can take him. He can't stand it when he looks at his iPhone and catches an unexpected glimpse of, say, Dave Letterman—his hero, only a couple of years older—his hair wiry straw, and the beard like a lunatic. Tom has to steel himself to sit and watch Dave's new Netflix show. Old man despicable me, he thinks as he watches Dave try to be cool with the likes of Kanye West. "You don't have to fawn. You're Dave Letterman!" he shouts at the TV.

It helps too that Tom's new girlfriend, Angela, is younger than he is. She entertains him, and now Bruno, with her crazy t-shirts. The shirts generally run to the *I'm Too Sexy (For My Shirt)* side of things. Though, the odd one she wears verges of vulgar. Like the one that stumped Bruno: *Caution I'm Slippery When Wet.* Bruno seemed to get the biggest kick out of the fact the logo was the same as the sign he puts in the lobby after he's washed the floor. Or maybe he was merely being polite. Tom couldn't tell for sure.

When he was a high school principal, he liked the Bruno sort, the diligent-not-too-bright-but-don't-underestimate-me type. Those students were excellent candidates for the tech stream—good with their hands in shop class—and dedicated to whatever they decided to pursue. Most of them grew up to be civic-minded, useful citizens. Better than the arty types who could gather a crowd to entertain, but ultimately sucked oxygen out of the room. The entertainers kept most of the good stuff for themselves. Never contributed unless they got back double.

Angela is different. She entertains but always gives back. Even the insignificant things, like when she broke the web on his old lawn chair horsing around, voguing to Madonna's song 'Hanky Panky'. When her foot crashed down on *Nothing like a good spanky. Good spanky...* she'd pulled out a rivet that held the strip of netting to the chair's frame. Afterward, she'd grinned at Tom and said, "Oops. Spank me." He loved that.

His ex, Vanessa, sits in the broken chair now. She and Tom are in the yard beside his suite. She shifts on the seat where the web is broken, and clucks her tongue every time a bit of her left cheek falls through the space where the netting has parted. As always, she is dressed to the nines. Tom is waiting to hear the reason for her visit. She's not the type to just drop around.

"Why do you keep this chair?" Vanessa asks.

Tom laughs. "It's vintage. From the 70s. I'll get one of those web repair kits from the hardware store."

"I don't think so. Not unless you pay a fortune on eBay. Nobody makes aluminum folding chairs anymore."

"Damn," he says. "Really?" Usually his pretending to be a clueless man gets a laugh out of Vanessa. Not today.

Truth is, Tom is in no rush to repair the chair. Angela will be over again, in some other silly glam outfit, to dance in the yard to whatever comes up on her playlist. The chair is her prop now. So different from Vanessa it makes him smile.

"Seriously, you should get this fixed. Or throw it out," Vanessa says. "Are you laughing at me?"

"No, I'm smiling because I know how much broken things drive you crazy. Why don't you sit here?" He gets up from the chair he's sitting on and motions to her.

"Stay where you are. I'll be quiet about it," she says.

He will tell Vanessa about Angela. He knows he owes it to her. He's waiting for the right moment. Or maybe he's chicken shit. Whatever the reason, the words are not ready to pop yet. How can this possibly be the moment to tell her he's met some-one at, of all places, a lawn bowling club? He'd been walking down at the waterfront when he came across the Kew Beach Club. Something about the manicured greens was so satisfying, he was drawn in despite his huge bias against it—his ninety-year-old aunt is a lawn bowler for God's sake. He'd gone up to the gate to get a better look when a large woman, in height and weight, came off one of the rinks. She was wearing a t-shirt with the slogan *Underestimate Me: That'll Be Fun.*

"Howdy. What can I do you for?" she'd said.

He laughed. He hadn't heard that corny opener in a long time. Even with the mask on he could tell she was younger than him, though she couldn't be that much younger. Nobody under sixty would be caught dead lawn bowling. Right? At his age Tom believed he'd be one of the youngest at the club if he were to join. When he inquired about membership, she said, "Sorry, dude. No new members until the pandemic is over. But if you come back in an hour, when the club is closed, I can let you have a try. See if you like it." She winked at him and he realized, Melissa McCarthy, taller but that's definitely who she looked like.

Something about her made him feel comfortable right off the bat, like he hadn't felt in years. When he returned an hour later, she showed him a few of the basics.

"It's simple, the object is to get your bowl closer than mine to the jack. The bowls have a weight bias. Little to the middle for a forehand." She points to a small logo on the bowl and lets it roll free toward the small white ball at the end of the green. Melissa, the only name he knew so far, was surprisingly light and elegant on her feet. He tried to imitate her and not only did he get his bowl closer to the jack than hers, but he smashed her ball into the ditch at the back.

"Bite me," she said.

With the expression Tom had an image of kids with head-phones in the school halls during the 1980s listening to The Flaming Lips. He prides himself on identifying people's eras by the language they use and the music that was popular at the time. He did the math in his head, but didn't believe it. Melissa couldn't be a serious lawn bowler and a high school student during the 80s. The two did not go together. She had to be older.

They did a few more bowls and Tom didn't want to leave.

"What happens if I hit the jack?" he asked.

"That's a toucher," she said.

"Oh I like the sound of that." He picked up another bowl and rolled it into the jack.

"A toucher," Melissa crowed. She started to dance on the grass singing, *Do you wanna touch, do you wanna touch, do you wanna touch me…*

"Suzie Quattro?" Tom asks.

"Joan Jett."

He joined her in the dance and the two of them twirled in their socially distant spaces in a fresh free way.

"This is fun, Melissa," he said.

She stopped twirling. "I get it. Another pretty, overweight woman. But my name is Angela."

That was a tough moment. He'd put his foot in it, but she didn't seem to hold it against him. She went back to twisting and swirling in her elegant way.

But this scene with Vanessa and the broken chair is not fun, is beginning to feel like torment. She's usually so direct about why she's visiting. Mostly she comes over when she wants to discuss something that's gone wrong in the house they once shared, or to ask his help with moving a piece of furniture she no longer wants, or to bring something she found of his that she thinks he might like to have back—like the rusted ratchet tool set she dug out from under the back stairs. Sometimes he wonders if she makes up reasons to come over, or is that just the arrogance of his having a new relationship?

"What's new?" he asks.

"Not much," Vanessa says. She shifts on the chair.

He's offered his own chair. He is not going to do that again. But this is confusing, she's sitting in a broken chair, saying essentially nothing. Maybe he should tell her about Angela. How he thinks he may have found someone he can settle down with, even though she is eighteen years younger. He'd confirmed the age thing when he'd played her one of his favourite songs, Earth Wind & Fire's 'Mighty Mighty', and she'd said, "We used to dance to this in kindergarten." He was already a young man in university when he first heard the song. If there's anything about the situation he doesn't like, it's that he is a *cliché*. He always swore he would not do the older man/younger woman thing.

Maybe it's the age difference that makes it too hard to tell Vanessa. Or maybe if he'd met Angela earlier, before lockdown. He senses Vanessa is having a hard time being single and what are the chances she's going to meet anyone now. He got lucky, and he knows it. Doubly lucky that it turns him on to watch Angela pull off her slogan shirt to expose one of her glam outfits underneath and dance to Beyoncé, Justin Bieber, or her favourite Bruno Mars, laughing at him when she's *waking up the rocket*. Something Vanessa would never have said or laughed about. Maybe she's even seen Angela out in the yard dancing with him.

She's got that perplexed look on her face like she is processing something, but is not sure how to express it.

"Not much. Not much happening these days," Vanessa says. "Still trying to write a little. Wrote a couple of poems this week."

"Oh good. Maybe one day you'll let me read one."

"They aren't very good. Kind of overwrought."

"Vanessa, you need to let that go. I am your friend. Not your critic. What do I know about poetry anyway? I'm only interested as a friend."

"I know. Thanks for the support, but that's not the way it works. It's too hard to explain. I should put away all the nonsense I write. Or at least leave it for me to read by myself at midnight."

This is going beyond. What is her problem? Clearly there's some reason she's here. Vanessa never goes into situations without a plan. Tom starts to get a bad feeling. Is there some sort of health issue? That would be terrible and hard for him to keep his spirits high. He's guilty enough as it is that life is good for him right now, and kind of lonely for her. For the first time he feels like he's met his match with someone who is attracted to him despite the fact that he is just Tom, a man who sometimes farts and burps, and isn't always dressed in the latest fashion. Someone who actually feels better if he's wearing clothing that won't be ruined if he slops supper on it. Vanessa of course looks beautiful as usual. She is wearing some sort of outfit she would describe as "this old thing", but he knows is expensive.

"I like your pant suit," he says.

"Thanks. The pants are Fendi stretch, and the jacket is repurposed. Got it for a song."

"Glad to hear it." He is not sure what Fendi stretch means but supposes it has something to do with the fact the pants are form fitting. Most people would call the jacket used, but knowing Vanessa repurposed means it's been deconstructed and reconstructed by some high-end designer. A buddy of hers in the industry probably did it. He admires how current she keeps her appearance, but is relieved he's no longer running along in the lane next to her in his stained windbreaker and dirty t-shirt. All the years they were together he was proud to be with such an elegant woman, but somehow he's finally grown up and become himself. He'd been over-married and in the end it hurt more than either of them expected when he couldn't keep up.

"I'm feeling pretty good these days," she says. "I thought I'd let you know…" A loud truck goes by and she stops talking.

"What's that?" he says. "Go on." But Vanessa is looking beyond him now.

"I think someone is coming to see you," she says.

He turns to see Angela has rounded the corner. She's not wearing glam today, although who knows what's underneath her baggy, grey sweatpants and stained sweatshirt. Today's shirt says *Don't Piss Me Off.*

"Oh, you have company," Angela says.

"You're early," Tom says. "Vanessa this is Angela. Angela—Vanessa."

"Pleased to meet you," Angela says. "I've heard lots about you."

"You have?" Vanessa answers.

"Angela and I are lawn bowling buddies," Tom says.

"Is that what we are?" Angela stares at Tom. "Actually, I didn't let him join the club."

"Okay this is awkward," Tom says. "Believe it or not, I was just going to tell Vanessa about you."

Angela makes a noise in her throat like a dog that thought it was going for a walk and got locked in the car instead. It's not exactly a whimper. It's part pissed off, part disappointed, and part snarl.

Vanessa smiles. The first real smile Tom has seen from her since she sat down on the broken chair.

"That's great," she says. "I'm glad you made a new friend, Tom."

He has to get his nerve up. As much as it might hurt Vanessa, he needs to stick up for himself and for Angela.

"Actually we're more than friends," he says. "We are starting to see each other." He knows he still hasn't said enough. "Like really *see* each other."

"Straight out love?" Vanessa asks.

"Love straight." Tom confirms. "No chaser."

Angela opens her eyes wide and makes a pucker with her lips. "Ah come on, at least a mixer. Please. Orange Crush is fun."

Everybody laughs but Tom feels a little hurt. Vanessa seems too okay with this. They couldn't stay married, he knew that. But he liked to think they were still an item of sorts. Or is he being a piggish man, now?

Vanessa stands to leave and Angela stands with her.

"You're not both deserting me are you?" Tom let's out a disappointed wail.

"Course not," Angela says. "I'm going to put the buffalo wings in the oven. You want to stay for dinner, Vanessa?"

"No thanks, but lovely of you to ask."

"Did you bring ranch or blue cheese dressing for the wings?" Tom asks.

"A special secret sauce." Angela throws her leg up and over the fence. Tom admires how agile she is, enough to get to the other side without opening the gate. Something even he with his tall legs can't do anymore.

Vanessa tugs at her Fendi skinny pants as she moves toward the gate. She opens it, passes through and waves goodbye from the far side. She heads in the direction of the house where they used to live.

After she is gone, Angela comes back out and says, "What a fancy lady."

"Takes all types to make the world go round," Tom answers.

"Some types don't go round so fast as they used to. Right, old man?" She laughs.

"Don't piss me off or I'll torpedo you." He makes a barreling bear hug move toward her. She holds him until he is finished with the deep snog he gives her neck. He likes that they are a physical match for one another. He can be his corporal self without fear of snapping her in half.

"I'm going to get a shirt made for you with that," she says. "*Don't Piss Me Off* across here." She draws her hand across the top of his chest. "*Or I'll Torpedo You* down here." She places her hand on his bellybutton. "Maybe an arrow pointing to the rocket? Too much?" She dissolves into laughter.

He can't help but feel turned on. He grabs her and they waltz around the yard together. How easily she moves with him in his arms. Like she trusts him. This feels too simple.

When the dance is finished and they are standing apart rearranging the lawn furniture getting ready for dinner, Bruno comes around the corner.

"What happened to that chair?" Bruno asks, pointing to the flagging piece of webbing.

"Ah. I'm a bit of a heavy foot." Angela laughs.

"If you're good with a different colour for that, I've got some webbing that should fix it."

"Great," Tom says. "I'll get it from you tomorrow."

"Want to stay for buffalo wings?" Angela asks.

"Sure." Bruno looks pleased to be included. "I'll sit over here. Social distance. Okay?" He holds his arms out like a kid about to helicopter.

"Love to have you," Angela says. "It's a hurt and dangerous world if we don't keep our pleasures simple."

She disappears into the apartment and one by one brings out a mound of wings, a bowl of potato salad, potato chips with sour cream dip, and a strawberry shortcake.

"A feast," Bruno says when everything is set up. As they eat, he starts to tear up. "It's been lonely this summer. Thanks for asking me. I have no one to talk to most evenings."

Tom is uncomfortable watching another man cry, even from six feet away. He puts his wing down on his plate and jams his hand in his pocket, smearing sauce on the leg of his pants. He wonders if this is where he and Vanessa had gone wrong. He tried hard to never let her see the slob he really is, and yet it seemed in the end that is all she could see. Or was it that she made it so it's all he could see about himself, and he was ashamed of it? Or maybe his inner slob simply had to get out and dance.

Angela jumps from her seat and says, "Dagnammit we're going to have ourselves a partay. Let's see what comes up on random."

She pushes her playlist button and smiles. "You're going to like this." Out of the Bose speaker comes Pharrell Williams singing 'Happy'. "Everybody, let's dance."

They skip, trip and hop in their spaces. Bruno jumps the highest.

Later in the bathroom when Tom takes the bar of Ivory soap to rub at the grease on his pants, he remembers Vanessa had something she wanted to tell him. He will find out what it is, but not now. He's unsure he can reach through anything more than 'Happy'.

Start Anywhere

On the walk home from Tom's, a towering vertical cloud splits the sky. To the north, a grey thunderhead fills with hail and lightning. To the south, the sun in brilliant blue sky reflects on the dangerous weather.

My duff is the sky. Scissored. Numb on one side. An exaggerated sense of a bum mushrooming on the other. Was it the broken chair or the silly new Fendi pants that killed half my ass? Stupid me. The whole time sitting in Tom's yard squirming instead of just spitting out what I'd come to say.

I twirl in front of the bedroom mirror.

The pants look okay if I hold my stomach in. But Jesus, the cupcake top if I let it out. Not a great look.

I lie on the floor, stare at the ceiling and try to meditate. I know I'm supposed to sit, to keep myself mindful—meditation is not the same thing as sleeping—but lying on the floor is not where I sleep. So it's all good. Right? Jive myself into believing whatever I need.

Be calm. Think nothing. Focus on breath… did I start to sweat when that woman Angela came by? Is that what happened? If not, then why didn't I notice how itchy these stupid Fendis can get before I paid $1000 for them? Was I in too much of a rush to get out of the change room at Holt Renfrew? Scared of germs? Scared of seeing the cupcake in a three-way mirror? Think nothing. Think nothing. Stop! Stop thinking about thinking nothing! Focus. But… why is Tom attracted to her? And that thing she was doing with her ass, is that what they call twerking? Am I disappearing into infinite little swipes of nothingness? A woman holding a mirror up to a mirror, vanishing bit by bit… Shut up, monkey brain. I'm trying to meditate.

I jump up. Rip at the Fendis with a couple of tugs of my arms, a jig with my feet, and fling them into the corner. An offering to the monkey brain. To make her shut up.

Stupid pants won't make me shut up. And by the way, Vanessa— I'm not 'monkey brain'. I have a name. I'm Cheeka.

Ignore.

Across the hall in the bathroom I find the magnifying mirror I use to search for chin hairs. I hold it up to my reflection in the hallway mirror. There are no infinite swipes. There's only one of me. And I am upside down, not disappearing into nothing.

Should you write a poem about this, Vanessa? No you should not. Karens don't write meaningful poetry. Go pluck some chin hairs.

Ignore, again.

Downstairs in the kitchen I decide to make an open-faced sandwich for dinner, but the bread is so mouldy I throw the loaf in the organics and start to eat smoked salmon out of the container with my hand. I pop bigger and bigger globs of pink flesh into my mouth, until the whole $11.00 worth is one greasy mound in my stomach.

You should have stayed for the buffalo wings.

Oh god, the thought of her making special sauce at Tom's for the wings with those rings on every finger was too much. Germ catchers. Especially the big, yellowed diamond with the tarnished claw setting on her middle finger. An engagement ring that belonged to her mother, or grandmother? How large must that woman have been? Pathetic, trying too hard—a scream to the world that she doesn't care if anyone ever marries her.

Tom might marry her. Who are you to put her down? Told you. You're a Karen.

Look I went over there with the best of intentions, to tell Tom I know he's seeing someone, and it's totally okay with me. *Liar. It's not okay. You just hope it will be, so you'll feel more optimistic about your own future.* No, I saw her dance routine in the yard by his apartment a couple of nights ago. And I know he digs her. I watched him put his arm around her neck and bury his face in it. Only Tom would get involved in a new romance during a pandemic. *Why not? If you're into it, you're into it.* Okay maybe the sight of it did loosen me up. Maybe his getting involved forced me to take a look at myself. Invigorated me enough to buy those stupid pants.

You know you feel sexy in them. Desperate pants in desperate times.

I only wore them to Tom's as a tryout. To ask if he thought they looked any good. All he did was blink like a mole caught in the sun and mumble, "I like your pantsuit."

Ha! You hoped he'd call them catch-me-fuck-me pants.

Screw off, monkey brain. Christ, isn't a woman entitled to a little peace in her own head?

Cheeka. The name is Cheeka.

Whatever, Cheeka. A reaction of some sort beyond "nice pantsuit" would have been appreciated. Clothing is important. It's that layer that separates us from the animals.

Bullshit. Your hands stink of salmon. You should be grateful to the salmon. Sleep on it.

I'm putting an amethyst under my pillow for protection against you, Cheeka.

Next morning, I start fresh. I retrieve the Fendis from the corner of the bedroom, shake them out and shimmy them up as far as I can get them past my hips. I lie on the bed to finish the job, roll off so the button at the waist doesn't pop, exhale to shrink my diaphragm, and bend over to zip up the cuffs. The button threatens, but hangs in.

Must be all that smoked salmon.

Forget it. The pants look hot and I'm going to the patisserie on Bayview in honour of a ritualistic gorge of smoked salmon by a sex-starved woman thankful to the fish for her supper. I might even snag a sidewalk seat at the shop since there's so many Nervous Nellies out there. Bye, Cheeka.

I'm good until I get to Bayview and see all the people wandering about without masks. I dodge the heavy mouth breathers—*Nervous Nelly*—and forge ahead. I really want that coffee and a sweet in the sun.

Admit it. It's the pants. They're charging you up, aren't they?

Okay I am charged, but I'm bummed to see all the sidewalk furniture piled in a heap in front of the patisserie. Same thing inside, the tables and chairs shoved in the corner with plastic wrap over everything. What good does that do? The damn virus can survive on plastic.

I stand six feet behind the man who is trying to show the barista a poster over the counter.

"Can't you make an exception for a good cause?" the man asks. "We need help, and it's Beethoven's 250th birthday."

The barista shrugs. "Not my policy. No exceptions. Not even for Beethoven. I have another customer behind you."

The man turns. He's cute behind his mask. When he walks past, I ask, "What's the cause?" I move toward him so he'll know I've engaged.

Too close. Too eager.

He steps back two meters and holds up the poster. "Can you read it? I don't want to hand it to you. You know with the whole no contact thing." He makes circles with his free hand as if he's clearing the air of cooties.

"Yes. I can read it. So you're with the Scarborough Philharmonic?"

"I am. Principal, second violin. It's a prerecorded concert we're Zooming this Friday as a fundraiser."

"I'll take a flyer if you have enough. Something to do. Almost like I have a date on Friday."

"You do. You have a date on Friday." He smiles and reaches across the distance to hand me the flyer.

I hesitate.

Take it, Nelly. You asked for it.

I snatch it, as if taking it fast will mean no germs pass, and I hear the words, "Can I buy you a macaron?" come out of my mouth.

Yeah. I had to get in there and vocalize for you.

"Sure," he says. His eyes look happy above the mask, almost like he might be interested. He turns to the barista and asks, "What flavours do you have?"

"Many. You know them," she says.

"Well that helps. How about coffee-flavoured?"

"Cappuccino or mocha?"

"Mocha."

"I'll have a lemon and a coffee," I say.

The barista puts on blue plastic gloves and moves toward the macaron case holding a pair of tongs away from her body as if she's about to deliver a baby. She pulls out a chocolate brown macaron and puts it on a sheet of baker's paper leaving it on the counter for the man to pick up. She takes another sheet, puts a yellow and a dark brown macaron on it for me.

"Sorry, I meant a lemon and a coffee to go," I say.

"That's what you have."

"No, I mean a coffee to drink." I don't want to hand everything back. It's been too much contact as it is, and the barista looks ready to explode. The point now is for me to complete this deal as fast as I can. I've got a stylish guy in a hip, lipstick-red athletic jacket waiting for me, and I'm here in my super-itchy, charged pants.

"Look. I'll take both macarons and a coffee to drink... to go... okay?"

Why are you asking permission? It's her job to sell you things.

"$17.50," the barista says.

I hold up my credit card and she shoves the machine at me. It's wrapped in saran and has grease and specks of icing on it. I push the buttons with the edge of my card, include a 25% tip, and tap. *You can't buy good behaviour. Does a dog stop barking when you give it biscuits? No. It's been rewarded for being bad.* The machine screeches a rejection. The man beside me seems transfixed. *Your ass is on show. What do you expect?*

I try again. Another screech.

"You'll have to insert the card," the barista says.

Against better judgment, I insert. We wait an interminable amount of time for the machine to churn out a ream of paper telling me the transaction is not approved. My hand is on fire now from touching all the things every other cretin who's been in the patisserie during the past week has touched.

Ew. You've got virus on that finger, Vanessa.

"I'll pay cash," I say.

"No cash."

"Well can you please try inputting again? I think the sale timed out."

"Allow me." The man is beside me now with his debit card extended. The barista snatches it from him, puts the sale through and hands him the machine to finish.

Outside the shop, the man and I awkwardly hold our pieces of baker's paper. I try to juggle my coffee so I can eat, but I can't manage it so bend to put the coffee on the sidewalk. The pants grip, distracting me, and I tip the cup to pour half the coffee out. A black swell forms around my feet. I think the man is smiling, though he hasn't taken off his mask yet.

"What a mess," I say. "Oh well, might as well eat one of these." I pull my mask down and hold the lemon macaron up thinking citrus blossoms and Mediterranean breezes. I bite into it and wince with too sweet and a distinct taste of aluminum. He smiles again.

"I know," he says. "The lemon is too powerful."

His mask is off now. I am too shy to really look, but catch a glimpse and see he is laughing because I have crossed my eyes. He might actually find me humorous.

Rock it.

"I'm sorry you had to pay after all that," I say. "I'll make a big donation to the symphony."

"Worth it then."

We stand with our treats. I shove the second one in my mouth whole so I don't have to feel tongue-tied for much longer, but it's worse now because I'm standing endlessly munching sticky sweet, and awkward silence happens anyway. When I finally swallow, I am babbling. "I like your jacket," I say. "Great colour against your skin. I mean, sorry... What am I saying? Umm... It looks good with your complexion. That's all I meant."

You're not supposed to comment on the colour of his skin. You don't know how to be with this, do you?

"Thank you," he says. "And your pants. Mighty fly."

"Really. You like them? I can't decide. I might'a got conned by a designer label."

"I know the feeling. I bought these because they're Versace." He pulls out a pair of oversized, red-framed glasses, and puts them on. I look at him properly for the first time and see he is strikingly similar to Spike Lee dressed to catch the eye of the paparazzi. Very cool looking guy.

"I dare you to tell me how much you paid. I want to know who's the bigger idiot paying for a label."

"Eight hundred without the lenses," he says.

"Ouch, but I win. A thousand!" I point to my pants.

"Wow. Who says this virus isn't making us crazy?" We both laugh in that friendly but not really sure it's a funny thing way.

"What's your name?"

"Leon. And yours?"

"Vanessa."

"Okay, Vanessa. See you this Friday on Zoom. There's a talkback after the concert. Join in." He hands me another flyer. "In case you have a friend you want to give it to."

He puts his mask back on. Immediately I want to see his face again. He walks to the corner, and turns to wave. "See you around," he calls.

I pick up my cup from the sidewalk, drain what's left of the coffee and take the cup inside to throw it away.

The barista is at the trashcan putting in a new garbage bag.

"Is it okay to dump the cup in the old bag?" I ask.

She looks at me and shrugs. I take this as a yes and toss.

"Check yourself," she says.

"Okay," I mutter, embarrassed and confused. I walk out the shop door and head toward home. It's not until I am by the Subway sandwich shop that I settle down enough to feel attacked and yet ignorant. Should I go back and apologize? But for what? I need more information. I am not sure what I did that needs checking.

It's not her job to explain to you what's going on.

God can't I just enjoy the day, Cheeka.

I turn the key in the front door to the house and go upstairs to lie on the floor in my bedroom. I place a blue quartz on my third eye for expanded awareness. I need to clear the anxiety around my ignorance and focus on a more creative and positive me.

What is it you want?

"To get these damn pants off," I say out loud.

I rip at them, ball them up and throw them in the corner. I dig in my cupboard to find my old yoga pants, the ones that are stretched and baggy in the knees, a bit too synched in the crotch.

Polite term for it. Those pants give you a camel toe.

"So what?" I say out loud again. I pull the yoga pants on, pick the lint from the shins, plop on the floor and take a deep breath.

On Friday evening when I sit at the computer, I'm still wearing the yoga pants and my old black cardigan. As I start to input the Zoom link from the flyer, my eye catches an item about the latest racially motivated police incident in Portland, and below it something about vaccines and failed trials. And I am off on a bout of doomscrolling that delays me by precious minutes into the concert. By the time I get back to it and join in, two men, one the music director and the other the concertmaster, are talking about Beethoven. How his music is an onion the listener needs to peel. The concertmaster says he's going to show us pictures that will help us know what mindset we should be in while we peel the onion.

The first is a photo of a young girl looking at herself in the mirror. The tune is supposed to make the listener feel imitation. *How do you feel imitation? Shouldn't it be reflection?* The music is by a composer I've never heard of before named Telemann. Four female violinists saw away in someone's tidy backyard while I search Telemann on my phone. He's a Baroque composer completely self-taught who became a musician against his family's wishes. Good for him, I think.

I search for the latest covid numbers on my phone, and miss what the next tune is called and what it's supposed to make me feel. But I hear the music director say, "We should all celebrate the opening eight notes." And from the first note, I am loving it. The full orchestra plays outside under a bandshell in a park that looks like a farmer's field. Everyone wears a black mask but I recognize Leon, even from above and behind, as the drone camera flies over the rim of his red glasses. When the drone comes down to face level, I see he plays with his eyes closed sometimes. I wonder if he closes his eyes for sex. The camera moves up and flies crow's view over the orchestra. The group sways like a soft breeze.

Turns out the tune is Pachelbel's 'Canon in D'. I should have known that. The concert goes on for another hour, and along the way we hear Hayden and Bach, a playful piece by Beethoven's friend Reicha—good to know the melancholy genius had friends—and finally a tune composed by Beethoven himself.

The music director tells us 'Opus 132' was written at the end of Beethoven's career, at a time when he was stone deaf and scared of dying. It's a quartet for two violins, a viola and a cello. Leon is one of the musicians. The quartet plays in someone's townhouse with a cleared out dining room that looks like it might have held an Ikea set. I expect the movement to be difficult and crashing, full of anguish and despair, which it is, but then there's a surprising nudge of joy.

Like life. Expect anguish but continue to find the joy.

The sound reduces slowly to a final note that is almost transcendental, leaves me unprepared for the return of the music director and the concertmaster who push for money, flash up buttons and links on how to make a donation, then through the magic of Zoom let us into the talkback.

Eighty-four of us participate. I scroll through the postage stamp faces in the gallery until I see Leon sitting in his living room. A candle flickers on a table in front of him. He looks sexy. Enticing, he appears to be alone. The words "check yourself" ring in my ears. But Cheeka hovers my hand over the Chat button at the bottom of the screen. She helps me locate Leon in the list of participants, and types him a private message: Great concert. Want to meet for coffee again?

I am riveted to the screen, not really listening to what anyone is saying. I check my own postage stamp face to be sure the light is flattering and my forehead is not too greasy. I tilt my laptop to create a filter effect and take the hollows out from under my cheeks. I have practically stopped breathing, while I wait for Leon to answer. A flag goes up on the Chat button. I jump on it, but it's only the symphony treasurer thanking everyone for attending. Then the concertmaster is thanking the director, and the director is thanking the donors, and the waning bits of digital life are bringing the talkback to a close. At the last second, a message to me says: Sure. Same place, ten tomorrow?

The host ends the meeting. My hand hovers on the mouse itching to say more, but with Zoom, when you're finished you're finished.

In bed, I close my eyes, try to will myself to sleep. A hundred deep breaths are supposed to help. I breathe in for a count of five, hold for five, breathe out for five. Twenty breaths in, and I begin to see myself floating away. I think it's the nether call of sleep until I realize it's light-headedness from holding my breath too long between repetitions. *This is supposed to relieve anxiety not induce it.* I sit up, take in a big breath and lie back down. How is it possible I am more wide-awake now than when I first lay down. In my crazy wakefulness I imagine my upside-down-self in the mirror again. The optics of this feel wrong. *Figure it out.* I find the magnifying mirror and hold it to my reflection in front of the hall mirror.

There's a reflection of a reflection, and as I walk toward the mirror my image flips upright. It's like the funhouse mirrors. This feels like some sort of progress. I lie back down. I put a rose quartz over my heart and a pyramid of apophyllite on my forehead.

Mini-temples of love and enlightenment. Now you're getting it.
Good night, Cheeka.

In the morning I yank on the old yoga pants, pick the hairs off my black cardigan, pull it on, take it off, put on the repurposed jacket, then take that off, too. I walk out the door in my old stripped t-shirt and yoga pants toward the coffee date. The anguished part of my wardrobe is looking to find joy in the day, but it feels like a pull-back to head for the patisserie again. I'm afraid of the barista and don't want her scowl to ruin the mood. So I'm happy to see a Closed sign in the window when I get there. I check the posted hours. The shop was supposed to have opened an hour ago. Being the anxious-on-time-therefore-too-early type, I have to hang around for ten minutes before Leon rounds the corner.

This is good. Gives you a chance to get calm and realistic about whatever this is.

When Leon is standing beside me, he says, "Wonder why it's closed? I could call my daughter and find out."

"Your daughter? Why?"

"She works here. She served us the other day?"

"That was your daughter? She's... I mean, ah... she doesn't look like you."

"Good thing." He laughs. "She's a woman and I'm a man. She's light if that's what you mean. And she's cranky with me right now because I broke up my marriage with her mom."

"Oh that explains it."

"Explains what?"

"I'll tell you over coffee. Let's get a Starbucks. I know a bench we can sit on if they've taken their chairs away, too."

We walk with our coffees down Millwood Road toward the Catholic School to sit on the bench near the front door. The coffee tastes burnt. I want to let Leon know I am a good person. Somehow I want to validate my missteps. Or at least make me not stupid. Not racist to have questioned anything about his daughter because she looks more white than Black. I want to tell him I grew up and lived in places that in too many ways made me ill-equipped to navigate. I want to tell him this not as an excuse but as an explanation as to why I am so terrified I am going to screw this up.

"I have no plan for how to do this," I say.

"You need a plan for this? We're having coffee."

"My whole life has been a series of plans. Not enough real thoughts. Only plans. I grew up believing if you don't have a plan, you waste your time. A very work ethic thing in me. You know umm… I was wondering… if we, you know… if we just…"

"If we just sit here and enjoy ourselves?"

"Yes, if I sit beside you and just enjoy. Is that okay?"

"It's a perfect day to have no plan. Start anywhere," he says.

CARE LESS

It's hard to know whether Aunt Marion heard what Vanessa asked. Her answer, "Not to be so careful," doesn't quite fit the question. So Vanessa repeats her question, extra loud. "What birthday wishes do you have?"

The scene is playing out like on countless news clips Vanessa has seen about the elderly, except Aunt Marion isn't being wheel-chaired in, she's walking unassisted into the dining room of the Westerly Parc. The nautical theme in the room, brass portal mirrors and net hangings, seems out of place in the sea of old people until Vanessa notices the coloured bits in the nets, and realizes they're wooden fish painted by the residents.

Everyone is assembled around the large chocolate cake decorated with yellow icing roses. HAPPY BIRTHDAY MARION 103 YEARS YOUNG is written in pink piping. People sing. Quietly. As if afraid they might disrupt the dead. Or maybe that's all the puff most of them have. A single candle waivers in the centre of the cake. It is meant to burn itself out. No blowing for fear of whatever might be in the ancient airways of the birthday victim.

"It's come to this. One candle. Protocol be damned." Marion disposes of the flame handily with an expansive blow. She looks pleased and tugs at her chignon, expertly repining the white hair on the top of her head for the photo opportunity. When the last shot is taken, she says, "To care less, Vanessa. That's my birthday wish for you."

"So nice," murmurs the female support worker who passes Vanessa a slice of cake. She, like most of the staff, is an Othered woman. This is a term Vanessa recently learned at her volunteer job with Shining Star—a program designed to help women get back into the work force. The people who run it have good intentions, but it seems inappropriate to make a distinction between those new to Canada and those born here. Yet the seminar leader up from head office in California insisted Othered is the preferred term.

Vanessa manages the clothing department for Shining Star. Every Wednesday and Friday she organizes the week's mound of donated clothing into batches: rack as is, mend, dry-clean, redonate, trash—it never ceases to amaze her how many donors think used pantyhose is something someone else might want.

And it is true most of the smiling people who keep the cheer, feed, toilet and support the residents at the Westerly appear to be relative newcomers. She wonders if the commissions and studies, and the sincere promises from the multiples of politicians, have had any impact on the working conditions of the people employed here.

She clucks her tongue thinking about it and decides to ignore what her Aunt Marion has just said. For one thing, she isn't entirely sure what part of her is too careful. As far as she's concerned she'd stopped being that way years ago, after she and Tom finally split. Still if she's honest, she has to admit she's felt a heaviness since he died two years ago. He'd never taken care with the melanoma first discovered on his head, refused to the end to wear a hat in the sun. He was a strong man with spirit, and now that he's gone, she misses having him just around the corner. His new wife, Angela, as was her right, took care of his memorial service. The event was oddly both too celebratory and too religious. Hard to tell which part bothered Vanessa more. And Angela had been there with a new man already, someone named Bruno. Even shared a dance with him at the reception. Since when was dancing part of a funeral? Her farewell speech included the old saw, "Better to get on with living than dying." It seemed crass in the circumstances, but Tom might have agreed.

Leon was gone, too, after they'd been together for more than twelve years. Toward the end, she'd heard his daughter tell him she thought Vanessa was a piece of work. As if she was a bolt of fabric randomly cut up and stuck with pins in a failed dress design. What had gone wrong with the design? People would likely line up to give their views on it if given a chance. But the truth is, Vanessa knew she'd killed the relationship before he left. She didn't want him to move in. Didn't want any man to ever move in again, just wanted a series of interesting visitors like Aunt Marion had all her life. And talk about being too careful, Leon went back to his wife at the end. Maybe people aren't supposed to break out of their boxes for long. Although that attitude is probably what Aunt Marion means about her needing to care less. She'll ask after the cake and tea are finished. For now she simply says, "Did you paint any of these fish, Aunt Marion?" She points to the closest sagging net full of colourful bounty.

"Mercy no," Marion says. "I'll show you later what I'm working on."

The support worker who brought around the pieces of cake ushers a young girl about seven or eight years old toward them. The girl carries a painting.

"This is Lily, my daughter," the woman says. "She painted these flowers for you, while she waits. She thinks you're nice."

"Gorgeous," Marion says. "I'll hang this in my bedroom."

"Where's your cane?" Lily asks.

Marion laughs. "Did you see me dancing the other day with my cane? I only use it when I'm dancing."

"Yes. You are a good dancer," Lily says. "I can dance." She pirouettes and stops to do a complicated unwinding that pops her arms, then her legs, and finally her torso in quick succession.

"Let me see if I got that right." Aunt Marion tries to imitate. She gets the arm pop, then freezes.

"Almost. Try again. It's hip hop." Lily slows the movement down. This time Marion follows the first two steps, before her body does a full cow shake sideways. Lily and Vanessa catch her, and everyone giggles.

"It's still okay to party at my age," Marion says, triumphant. "I'm learning to hip hop."

"Oh good," Lily says. "Hip hop is my favourite. Jheric is my teacher on the days I don't have to come and wait for Ma."

"Why do you come to wait?" Vanessa asks.

"Nobody at home. Lots of jobs. Right, Ma?"

Ma answers with a vague, preoccupied smile. Vanessa feels like something more should be said or done, but has no idea what that something is. She looks at Lily's Ma and says, "My name's Vanessa."

"Josie," the woman says.

"Nice to meet you."

After the party breaks up, Josie steers Lily toward a chair in the lobby. When Vanessa and Marion head out of the dining room and pass by, Josie is saying, "Be patient. Ma won't be much longer." Lily sits on the chair and swings her legs with that little girl look that says she wishes she was doing almost anything but sitting in an old age home waiting for her mother to get off shift.

It's the first time Vanessa has visited Marion since she finally moved into her own room at the Westerly. She'd made it to a hundred and two in the house, then decided it was time, mostly because Vanessa, her only remaining relative, lived miles away and at seventy-six was no longer a kid herself.

The idea of the move gave Vanessa an ache in her throat, like she'd swallowed a giant chicken bone that wedged sideways. She still feels it when she thinks about it. Marion had always thrown her doors open wide whenever Vanessa needed it. The house, which Marion had inherited from her mother, had been one of the few constants in Vanessa's life. Her only real home.

The day before Marion was scheduled to leave, the Westerly had called to say her room wasn't ready as expected.

"Somebody didn't die on cue I guess," Marion had said.

"Did you tell them you're all ready to go?" Vanessa asked.

"I didn't. I didn't think it through. The call caught me off guard."

So Vanessa got on the phone and called the Westerly, but management couldn't or wouldn't tell her what the problem was. They did at least agree Marion could move into their respite room until hers was ready. When Vanessa told Aunt Marion this, she'd asked, "What's a respite room?"

"I don't know. I didn't think it through, either." Vanessa laughed, though nothing was funny about the situation.

Everything about the move felt unreal and logical thoughts were not coalescing for either of them. She should have called back to ask about the respite room, because Marion ended up staying for two months in a room that felt more like a departure lounge than a bedroom—plastic chairs, plastic bedside furniture, and plastic blinds that clacked in a draft.

But Marion had been brave when the time came to leave her home. She'd walked out of the house, locked the front door, and climbed into Vanessa's car.

"I'll bring joy to this if it kills me," she'd said as she settled in the front seat. She was more or less a natural at generating joy, but even her reserves were tested that day. The two of them had decided the house should not be sold right away. Marion might want to come back on weekends—something that hasn't happened yet—and Vanessa in her heart wondered if she might move in herself. What had gone unsaid between them was that in truth, it was a lot easier to leave everything in place than it was to go through the process of clearing out as if Marion might never return. How were they to throw out her tangerine stilettos, her jumpin' jack flash velveteen tights, her polka-dot bikini?

A stack of Marion's more proper clothing, what she called her *old lady things*, and a cache of her best art supplies were piled on the back seat of Vanessa's car the day she moved. Before pulling from the curb, Vanessa turned to make sure everything looked secure. It unnerved her how much the scene resembled the one from sixty-five years earlier when Aunt Marion had picked her up after school—her own fuzzy turquoise bathrobe wrapped around her underpants, her best dresses around her socks, and the green Frisbee her father had given her plunked on top.

After that day, Vanessa had stayed with Marion for the rest of the school year and all of the next while her parents tore each other's lives apart. The house is a tidy stone and brick bungalow off the Kingsway. It doesn't look like much from the outside, nor did it on the inside when Vanessa's grandmother lived there, but once Marion got hold of it, the house started to fill with treasures. In every cupboard and on every shelf fantastic mementoes from her adventures: cowboy boots, peacock feather fans, French bustiers, a poster signed by Jimi Hendrix with the words *great time* scrawled under his name, a jeweled skull from Haight-Ashbury, a black selenite wand from Brazil. And the centerpiece, a brilliant orb of orange and yellow calcite that glows like an Ontario sunset in late August. "Keeps all who look at it from burning out," Aunt Marion said. Sometimes on the weekends, the two of them would light incense and place all the crystals and quartz on the coffee table to play with the Ouija board. At the end of the night, especially if it had been a scary one, like the time the wand spelled *death by horror facelift* and the neighbour's Doberman came snarling at the back door, they'd spit on a piece of amethyst to ground themselves and clear the negative energy.

Vanessa didn't move back in with her mother until she was in a *stable situation*. These are the words the adults used to mean she'd met another man. The house her new stepfather owned, a substantial red brick two-storey in west Toronto, never felt like a home, though he did try in his straight-laced engineer's way to be a good parent. Part of the problem was that he was too old to be a dad who wanted to play in the yard, or go to the beach, or to do anything much on the weekend but sit in a chair and read. Strange no one ever thought Vanessa could or should have moved in with her father. Maybe if she'd ended up in New Mexico with him, she would have loved her life better. Or maybe, it would have been dreadful. She realizes now her father had been a handful, and she misses her mother more than she ever expected. She wishes she'd tried harder to make things fun for her, perhaps even invited her and her stepfather to play Ouija.

A couple of miles out on the drive toward the Westerly, Marion had said, "I think I forgot something. Can we stop look in the art box?" Vanessa found a parking lot to pull into and retrieved the box from the back seat. She stood at the side of the car with it open while Marion moved things around in it.

"It's not here," she said.

"What's not here?" Vanessa asked.

"My watercolour set. Nice Winsor & Newton paints. I wonder if I threw them out by accident?"

"I'll look next time I go back. If I can't find it, I'll buy you a new one." Vanessa hoped this would do. She didn't have the energy to return to the house so soon after they finally got out the door. But she should have. The rest of the drive to the Westerly she felt like a con. She tried to tell herself Aunt Marion didn't really paint much anymore. But she knew it was a lie, part of the magical thinking she did around difficult things to make them easier to accept.

When they get to Marion's room at the end of the hall, Vanessa is glad to see the furniture she'd sent from the house is set up including some of the beautiful art, and the life-affirming orange calcite orb on her bedside table by the window—it's taken on a ruby grapefruit glow from the sunlight. Marion's self-portrait as nude painted in the 1960s hangs over her bed. She did have a spectacular figure. To this day, Vanessa can't look at the painting for long without wondering when staring turns to voyeurism, and a jealous desire to have led Marion's life creeps in.

Vanessa doesn't like that the room has a faint odour. If the smell could be bottled, a critic would say: *a young bleach with notes of medicine, urine and citrus.* And the chairs, except the recliner which she assumes Marion will sit on, are piled with clothing, all the hangers missing. She isn't sure where to sit until Marion points to the sliding glass door and says, "We can go to the balcony. This room still stinks. Dare I say from the last resident? I asked them to take my clothes out of the cupboard until the smell disappears."

Vanessa smiles. She will bring the cleansing selenite wand next time she comes.

"I brought another one of your watercolour sets," she says. "I found three of them."

When she'd searched for the watercolours, she'd also found a box of her father's things that had somehow ended up with Marion. Going through the contents was like mining the past. Inside was the Bick's gherkin pickle pin he'd picked up as a kid at the Canadian National Exhibition and sometimes wore on his

lapel telling people he was a member of a secret club (the Fickle
Pickle Spy Network). She also found the Dracula teeth he wore
at Halloween to scare the trick-or-treating kids, and the piece of
lavender paper with the 'All You Need Is Love' sticker on it.
Looking at the paper, she realized finding it the first time was
when she knew her parent's marriage was falling apart. The iden-
tity of Rambling Rose who'd signed it is a mystery he'd taken to
his grave. At the bottom of the box there was a list her father had
written in pencil titled 'Stuff Worth Living For':

Smell of fresh mown lawn
Early morning on the road
A flock of wild turkeys at the old house
A vixen and her kits under the porch
My grandmother's porridge—
brown sugar, fresh cream & raspberries from Mr. Norman
Smell of my Dad's neck
Watching my mother play piano
Listening to her sing Ladybug, Ladybug Fly Away Home
Holding hands with my love
Unconditional hug from Vanessa

She knew her mother was not the love on his list. "Little
things in a person mean a lot," he once told her.

"Some of the staff are embarrassed to look at that." Marion
points to her self-portrait. "Why not hang it? It was good then.
Lots of fun… It's fun now." She walks out onto the balcony.
Vanessa follows. There's only one chair on the balcony, but
Marion holds her hand toward the chair and beckons Vanessa
with her eyes to sit.

"I'll stand," Marion says.

"Really?"

"Really. I can feel all my parts when I stand."

"That's exciting."

"Thrilling actually."

After a time, Vanessa feels stupid and guilty sitting in the
only chair. She jumps up but her knee reacts, throwing her

back into the seat. "It's a trick making my knee work," she says.

"Come inside then," Marion says. "I want to show you something anyway."

She sits on the recliner and points to the coffee table they used to play Ouija on. Vanessa thinks she can still find the board in the house. Now, there's a small cracked ceramic jug on the table. Pencils and a paintbrush are stuck in it. Beside the jug, a couple of sketchbooks. "Bring those books here," Marion says.

Vanessa sits on the bed beside the recliner when Marion opens the biggest book to a pencil sketch. A little shaky, at first hard to recognize, then Vanessa sees it. A flaccid, circumcised penis with what would be a cliché to say except that they are— pendulous balls.

"It's a gesture sketch," Marion says. "He stood for this one. I was out of practice. Don't worry. They get better." She keeps turning pages. The drawings show more belly and chest as they improve.

Vanessa has no idea what to say. Marion stops on a sketch, and says, "He was sitting in this chair. It just sort of nested there like a hedgehog. Kind of cute, don't you think?" She laughs and Vanessa does, too.

She flips the page and sets the pad on the bed beside Vanessa. "This is the best one. It's the one I want to paint properly."

The sketch has a dark sienna wash on the torso. "He's Egyptian," Marion says. "Ahmet."

"His name?"

"Yes. Ahmet Elias."

"Nice."

"He's younger. Ninety-nine. But in some ways older."

"What do you mean?"

"He fusses. Worries what his kids will think. I tell him, you should laugh over them not cry. But he doesn't always listen."

"Do you think one of his kids might be named Rudy?" Vanessa has not intentionally changed the subject. But she isn't sure where to go next with the topic of no kids, and she'd gone to school with a boy named Rudy Elias. She remembers him to do this day because everyone used both his first and last name whenever they spoke about him. He was a gentle boy. Seemed kind. A quality Vanessa admires more and more as she ages.

To Marion having no kids meant she got to travel the world, do what she wanted. To Vanessa it's tied to some unused part of herself, a deficit. A plan that hadn't gone right starting with the abortion. Her doctor told her the scarring from the infection provided a natural birth control. "Nothing's *ever* going to get through there," he'd said, as if it was something she should be proud of. She hates that she partly agrees with the people who think a woman can be a world leader, but if she doesn't have kids she's failed in some way.

"Yes," Marion says. "He might have a son named Rudy. I think I've heard that name." Then as casually as if they'd been looking at pictures of kittens and puppies, she flips the page in the book and says, "Here's a new friend."

An uncircumcised penis, slightly longer, and somehow more independent looking, stares back at them.

"What happened to Ahmet?" Vanessa asks.

"Heart attack—supposed to be back next week—we'll see if it still works." Marion smiles.

Vanessa had not anticipated this answer. "Oh I'm sorry. I hope he's okay."

"Yeah. Me too. I like him." Then Marion flips to a sketch of the ceramic jug on the coffee table with a cobalt wash. "I did this one in the art class. The cracks look good. I was worried about getting them right. The jug's still useful."

"True. Sometimes I wonder how a person stays useful?"

"There's always someone who can use your help. I need your help, sweetie."

"I know. I have to reset my finding a purpose in life button. You remember what Dad used to say, 'Reset or flame out'."

"You'll find it. Dig in and stop focusing on the cracks."

Marion wrenches them out of the conversation by getting out of her recliner and shooing Vanessa off the bed. "I need to lie down before chair yoga. Could have fooled me I'd like yoga. Ahmet got me into it. Maybe you can meet him next time."

"I hope so. Do you want a blanket?"

"No. I'm good."

It takes Marion a few seconds to get settled and then almost immediately she looks to be asleep, so it surprises Vanessa when she opens her eyes and says, "And smile. That's important. It exercises the happy part of your brain."

As Vanessa walks down the hall, she does start to smile. It's then she decides she will get that tattoo she's been thinking about. A tiny pink crayfish like the one on the shoulder of the young woman she'd seen playing in the waves at the Beaches. Crayfish are brave, she thinks. The eyes on the end of their stalks never stop searching, even when something or someone has them in a grip.

Josie and Lily are still in the lobby. "Your aunt," Josie says, "she is so nice. We love her."

"Me too," Vanessa says. She gets to the front door and turns. "Don't be afraid to shout…"

She had intended to add *if Aunt Marion needs anything.* But she leaves it midsentence. Who is she to add herself to the mix of people Josie must look out for? Besides an encouragement to shout might be useful. It's a start toward the something more that should be said or done.

By the time she gets to the parking lot, she decides she will break Aunt Marion out for a weekend back at the house. They'd kept it for a reason. Maybe they'll even bring Ahmet with them. Put out all the crystals and the quartz and play with the Ouija board. What would Rudy Elias from the old neighbourhood think about that?

Acknowledgments

There are many people to thank. Here are some of them.

To my mom, MN Ruth, my sisters, Patricia and Beth, and my cousins, Linda and Marion, for their love and inspiration.

To school friends, Jane x2, Kitty, Mary Ann, and Denise, who stalk the halls of some of these stories.

To Darcy for his serious, sensitive read.

To Carina for cheering me on, this time from her back patio.

To Lanky ShankZ (Al) for his spirit that makes music.

And to Jeff for not once snapping when I asked, "Can you read this, again, to see if I got it right?"